HAPPY FOR YOU

Love & Family #3

ANYTA SUNDAY

First published in 2019 by Anyta Sunday,
Contact at Bürogemeinschaft ATP24, Am Treptower Park 24, 12435 Berlin, Germany

An Anyta Sunday publication
http://www.anytasunday.com

ISBN 978-3-947909-15-5

Cover Design: Natasha Snow

Line Editor: HJS Editing
Proofreader: Lynda Lamb

This book contains sexual content.

Chapter One

FELIX

THESE DAYS, I'M ALWAYS IN THE GROOVE.

Not enthusiastic footwork *in the groove*—too uncoordinated for that—nor doing anything exceptionally well *in the groove*. I'm in The Groove, my ancient 1988 Holden Commodore.

Pimped out with wood paneling and vinyl seats, she was named by my dance-crazy siblings because half the time we're riding in her, we're headed to dance classes.

Like Tiffany's dance class.

Which we should be heading to now.

Where are my sisters?

I honk, lean over the sun-warmed console, and roll down the window.

My home—childhood and current residence—winks in the afternoon sunshine. The vertical red paneling and tin roof create a barn-like effect. Cabbage trees shroud the upper windows, and a well-trod brick path curves through wild lavender. Hills rise behind the house like a cresting wave. Bordered by native bush, a tadpole-infested stream runs through our back yard.

I call out to the girls and Tiffany responds with a muffled, "Coming."

DJ Dangerfield's energetic radio voice fills the car. Music always eases the race against time, and if I can coax the girls to sing along, even better.

I'm hoping for some upbeat Pax Polo—

"Yesterday" tinkers softly.

The notes slam memories of *him* into my chest.

I fumble and change the station, but the song echoes in my head. I tug at my bow tie and work my mouth into a smile. It aches, but at least it'll look real to my sisters.

Tiffany slides into the passenger seat, her dark, wavy hair pulled into a bun. A rosy flush brightens her gently-freckled cheeks. "The twins are hiding from you," she murmurs.

She eyes the dashboard clock. Tiffany's class starts in twenty-five minutes.

Crap. "I'll be *one* minute."

I race inside our house, sneak past Mum asleep in her room, and throw open the door to my nine-year-old sisters' bedroom.

"Gah. It's Felix!" April and May are a dark-headed blur as they shove open their window and simultaneously swing their legs over the sill.

"Get back in here."

They stop. With a gulp, they glance at each other and turn dazzling smiles on me.

I'm not buying it.

I lift a brow. "Butts outside. Tiffany's waiting."

Buckled up and rumbling down the road, I eye the twins in the rearview mirror.

May cracks. "If you're gonna tell us off about the glow-worms, we can explain."

I glance at her identical accomplice. They're wearing white button-down shirts tucked into jeans, bright green Chucks, and bow ties. They adopted my style last month, and it makes my chest twist every time I see them.

I blink back the rush of mixed feelings and adopt a firm voice. "By all means, explain."

They blurt out their excuses. "The larvae looked like bioluminescent pearls."

"We thought they'd look good around mum's neck. Give her a real glow."

"Which was why we turned her light out first."

Tiffany and I exchange disbelieving looks. I say dryly, "Naturally."

"Of course, that meant we needed flashlights," May says.

April stares thoughtfully outside. "I guess all the arranging around her neck killed them."

May hums in agreement. "That, or mum's scream."

My sisters' imagination is frightening—good luck to anyone who breaks their hearts.

I pin them with a prompting look through the rearview mirror. "And . . ."

"We feel sorry?"

I twirl a finger. "Keep going . . ."

"And we'll keep the light on next time?"

I pinch my nose.

May delivers me a smile that isn't half as reassuring as she thinks it is. "Okay. You'll never catch us doing that again."

They must think I'm an idiot. "*Don't* do it again."

Construction ahead; I ease up on the gas and prepare to merge lanes. The twins' conspiratorial whispers trail to the front. "Do you think Felix—"

"—would look prince-like with a glowing crown? Hell yes."

I shake my head, a grin tugging my lips. Mental note: lock my bedroom door at night.

A car careens from behind and overtakes right when it's my turn to merge. I brake, and Tiffany's chest bumps the hand I whip out.

"You okay, Tiff?" I check the twins in the mirror. All okay.

Holy crap. What a bastard driver.

"This is why I never want to drive," Tiffany says.

"Oh, Tiff. Don't put this on your con list."

"Well, it's not going on the pro list."

Cars zoom past in the single lane, no gap in sight. No one lets us in.

Tiffany sighs. "I'm not going to make it in time."

A famous international ballroom dancer is running a guest session today—something Tiffany has been looking forward to all month.

"Lauren won't let him leave without meeting you," I say softly. "And if he does leave, then I'll become an internationally famous dancer and give you the lesson myself."

She snickers.

There's no making a dancer out of me, let alone an internationally famous one. I'm the only one in our family who didn't inherit the dancing gene.

Mum tried to teach me the basics, but she gave up when I turned fourteen. Around the time the twins were born. Around the time Dad left us. Around the time I started noticing my brother's best friend.

I hurtle into a free slot in the traffic. The second lane soon opens and I press down on the gas.

Hope lights Tiffany's brown eyes.

We race along the bays. I imagine we're sailing over glittering waters toward Wellington Harbor.

God, I love driving. The Groove, a steadfast and reliable

keeper of laughter, stolen tears, and whispered secrets; a confessional for Tiffany, April and May. Me.

Lights flash, followed by the familiar sound of sirens.

Blast it all to hell.

"Third time you've been pulled over this year." April sings from the back seat, "You're gonna get in trouble."

Deep trouble.

Tiff stirs uneasily, and I settle a reassuring palm over her forearm.

The last thing I want to do is reveal that I'm nervous. That I've accrued too many demerit points on my license—bad luck more than recklessness—and I can't afford more.

Please, please, please. Don't suspend my license. I need *to drive.*

"Let's see if we can't charm our friends into a warning," I say, forcing brightness into my voice. "Happiness is infectious, crew."

"Happiness is infectious, alright," May mutters with a snort. "Them cops look gleeful."

I choke the steering wheel, slip on a wobbly grin, and wind down the window. "Good afternoon, officers . . .."

Chapter Two

MORT

It's tough to ignore the fear prickling my gut as I hustle through the crammed arcade to Roch. My best friend. Or at least, he was once.

He's sitting at our old booth—the one that connects the arcade to the dance studio.

Roch sits tall on a crimson bench. Dressed in a tight shirt and black pants, he's pouring hot sauce into a paper tray of fries. His dark hair is cropped the shortest I've seen it.

He pops a fry into his mouth and checks his phone. His expression morphs from pensive to glowing.

I sling myself onto the sticky bench. "What's the secret to a smile like that?"

His gaze jerks to me. "Love and hot sauce."

For a moment, it's like the last year never happened. Like we're picking up where we left off.

Roch soaks me in, from my casual unbuttoned shirt, sleeves shoved around my elbows, to the cap settled low on my head.

His smile fades. "It's strange seeing you again. Same lazy smile, same dimpled chin, same ache in your eyes."

It's not the same ache though. This ache is a direct result of the last year.

Roch is all hard lines as he leans forward, frowning. "You wanted to meet? Why?"

No niceties for us. No bullshit. Straight to the point. "Can I order a drink first?"

Roch slides his soda across the shiny metal table.

"Cheers, Roch."

"Michael."

I bury a wince in a long, slow gulp of sparkling water. He's never been Michael to me. For as long as I've known him, his family and I have called him Roch—*rock*—an abbreviation of his family name, Rochester. "Michael."

Roch's voice pinches. "It's been twelve months."

Twelve miserable months that were the biggest mistake of my life. "I sent you emails."

"Christmas and birthday. Each one felt like a slap."

I fucked up all right. "I'm sorry."

I spin the glass, condensation wetting my fingers. The awkward silence makes my stomach clench. Our silences used to be easy. Never like this.

I gesture toward the tunnel. "Did you come from rehearsal?"

"I'm taking a season off. Tiffany's in a lesson."

So many questions. "Is she competing yet?"

"You're not here for an update on ballroom dancing."

I hunch forward, planting my elbows on the table. "I, ah . . . How's your mum after the transplant?"

"Not suffering kidney failure anymore."

Grief and guilt torpedo through my chest. I'd given up my best friend and his family over a few painful words. I should have returned sooner. Better yet, I should have stayed in Wellington. Fought for Roch. Fought for my place in the Rochester family.

Instead I spent the time teaching in Dunedin, writing unsent emails to the Rochesters and making up excuses not to come home.

I reposition the cap on my head and side-eye the arcade. Colors pulse, bright yellow and blue with flashes of red. Jerky clangs and echoed bleeping fill the spaces between teenage snickers.

The bulky Dance Dance Revolution machine hasn't moved an inch in a decade. The only place more meaningful we could have met is the station wagon I passed on to his brother.

I breathe in tepid air and tender memories.

The arcade and dance studio was our old turf. Our high school stomping ground.

Every day, after class and on weekends, Roch and I were here. He would practice ballroom dancing with his dance partner Lauren, and I'd study kinematics and thermodynamics on the sidelines. He'd snicker at me for being a geeky jock. I'd return the favor by calling him the most dapper straight guy of the millennium. The moment dance practice ended, we headed to the arcade and indulged in our own dance competitions, belting out Lady Gaga's "Bad Romance" lyrics as we jumped on the floor pads.

My throat tightens. "Remember when we came here on your eighteenth birthday?"

Roch glances toward the machine. "Broke in here, you mean."

"We had a key."

"That we stole from Lauren's mum."

I grin. "We danced all night."

"You wouldn't leave until you'd beat my score."

"Which I did."

Roch shakes his head, lips twitching. "We're still the top scorers."

He'd checked recently? Thought about us? I swallow. "I missed you. You, and the twins, and Tiffany. And . . . Felix." God, Felix. A whole year, I haven't heard his smooth voice as he whips out quick retorts. A whole year, I've been starved of his oblivious touches—on my arm, neck, shoulder, stomach, thigh . . . "*Really* miss you."

Roch presses his lips together. He sinks back in his seat and sighs. "You always were slow to realize your feelings."

Not to realize them. Just to announce them. I readjust my cap, unable to meet his eyes.

"How long have you been back in Wellington?"

I scrub a hand over my stubbly jaw. "Almost two months. Just before Dad passed away."

Roch looks unsure whether to offer sympathy or share relief. I spent ninety percent of my time sleeping at his house, so he knows better than anyone that my dad was a Class A bastard.

His voice breaks. "You handled it alone?"

"Asking you to help deal with my shit couldn't be the reason to start over with you."

"Start over? Is that what you want?"

I lean forward, hook his gaze. "More than anything."

Roch's eyes shimmer and he blinks. "Where are you living?"

"Blakewood Ave."

"You've been living . . . Christ. The entire time? *Two minutes away*?"

"I avoided your street."

"Why?"

"Dad died and I didn't forgive him. The moment he passed, I regretted not giving him his last wish. Since then, I've wondered if you Rochesters would ever forgive me. I was too afraid to find out."

"Until today."

My words come out broken, "I'm still afraid."

Roch frowns.

Don't ask me to leave. Don't.

"Mort—"

"Tell me about you—the family. How are you?"

Roch considers me a moment and then nods. "Felix's license got suspended. It's been chaotic, driving him and the girls around between work and wedding preparations."

My breath sticks in the base of my throat. "You're getting married?"

"End of summer."

"Wow." It feels like someone's juicing me dry. My best friend is getting married and I didn't know. "Congratulations."

Roch smiles dreamily. "Lauren's the best thing that ever happened to me."

Roch is engaged. To *Lauren*. "You two got back together."

"Even when we weren't dating, she never left my side." His gaze is hot and pointed. "I know a happily-ever-after when I see one."

My voice comes out crackled. "I'll fix us."

Roch snags back his drink. "It's not just me. You broke the family when you left. Everyone but Felix. Impervious Felix. But then, you never could do wrong around my brother."

I'll fix things. I want to be part of this family again.

Roch's eyes glisten like he can read my thoughts. Like he wants the same but doesn't know if it will work.

He checks the time. "Almost time for the engagement party."

I wish I could be there, but considering everything . . . "Maybe I can come around tomorrow? Help clean up?"

He finishes his drink and stands. His focus flits to our old corner of the arcade. "The party starts at six. Come any time after that."

He walks away and I snag his wrist. He looks at me, pained and hopeful.

"I fucked up, Roch—Michael. I want you to be happy I came back." I reluctantly let him go. "I want to be at your wedding."

Chapter Three

FELIX

Six months suspension.

I bang my forehead against The Groove's hot metal roof. The wagon is jammed between Roch's BMW and Mum's permanently stationary Honda. Even if I could legally drive, there'd be no getting her out.

The metaphor for my life doesn't escape me. Boxed in. Unable to do what I want . . .

No, wait. I need to be optimistic. Maybe the wagon represents safety. It's my bubble, protecting me from messing up. Where I'm living life well. Where I'm . . . happy.

Right. Yes. That. Totally that.

A chorus of music and laughter sails from the back yard.

Enough hiding. I push away from the car and lift my chin.

At the side of the house, I bump into the twins sneaking away from the party.

May blurts, "We're heading to the park."

Her and April's eyes glitter brighter than the sequined bow ties they donned for Roch and Lauren's party. I know mischief when I see it, and these two petite, wild-haired, science-crazy girls are embodiments of it.

The park. *Riiiight.* "Leave the glowworm cave alone."

The girls share a look that says *muahahaha.* I roll my eyes, and when I refocus, they've zipped past me. Our gate needs a sign: *Beware of Small Stealthy Scientists.*

I circle picnic tables, pass Roch and Lauren waltzing under a canopy of roses, and head for Tiffany. She's leaning on the bouquet-fringed bridge.

A pine-scented breeze makes her gold dress shiver.

"Does Mum know you're wearing her clothes?"

Tiffany stares at the stream. "She would if she were out here."

I rest my forearms against the rough wooden rail and watch our reflections on the surface. "She'll come out soon." I nudge her elbow. "Want to shove me around the dance floor?"

She peeks at me. "You need lessons. It'd make Roch and Lauren super happy if you managed a waltz at the wedding."

It might make everyone happy to see me dance—for the rarity of it. If I could pull it off flawlessly, I might be their momentary hero. "Will you teach me?"

"If you find another pair of feet to trample." She wiggles her toes in her sparkling slippers. "I need mine for competitions."

I hitch a thumb at my chest. "Hooking a toe donor for this charity case? No sweat."

"Will your toe donor also be your plus-one?"

I stiffen. These kinds of conversations sting.

I drum my fingers over the rail, and jerk them back at a splinter.

Admitting that I don't have a plus-one—for the wedding, and possibly for life—gets me all kinds of miserable.

The side gate snaps loudly in a lull between songs, and my focus slides to the new arrival—

Electricity bolts through me, painful and aching, until I'm so fried I can't feel. Can't think.

The music and chatter sound distant, muted by the ringing in my ears.

I know that figure. That cool, casual gait. That cap. His image taunts me every time I close my eyes.

Mort Campbell. Staring at the grass-choked bricks, lavender shoots snatching at his legs and tramping boots.

I blink, and blink again. I'm imagining him.

He's a figment of my exhausted mind.

He must be.

In a haze, I hustle through foxtrotting dancers toward him. "Mort."

He stops at my shout and lifts his head.

His face is exactly as I remember it: cleft chin, sharp nose, day-old stubble. Hazel eyes trained on my face, searching my expression.

I halt in front of him. "You're here?"

He reaches out to hug me. Like he might have a year ago. "Hey, Felix."

I swat his arms away. I don't want a hug. I want proof this is really him. I run my index finger over the mole on his throat. His pulse hiccups under my fingers.

"Felix?"

His low, rumbly voice is like a river lapping at a pebbly shore. It invades me, spiraling shivers from scalp to toes.

My fingers shake as I pull frantically at his neatly-ironed, safari-style shirt. One button pops off and drops into a lavender bush.

"Felix?" His breath fans over my nose and rolls to my cheekbone.

I drag my fingers across his wiry chest hairs to the flat

freckle at his right pec. His nipple is warm. He certainly *feels* real.

I undo the metal button of his cotton-twill shorts.

His firm grip stays my hands, and a curious frown bores into me. "What are you doing?"

"You must be an apparition."

A soft chuckle curls around me. My heart thumps.

"And opening my pants will prove I'm flesh and blood?"

I grind my teeth against the sting rising up my throat. "You must be an apparition, because Mort Campbell died a year ago. When we were in hospital. When he wasn't with us."

Mort's eyes shutter closed and he swallows.

"You must be an apparition because Mort was smart. He'd never stroll back into our lives at Roch's engagement party with a cavalier 'Hey, Felix.' I jut my chin toward his pants. "Open them."

"Shit, Felix." His expression teems with regret. His grip loosens on my wrists. "I'm sorry."

I smile as I pinch the zipper and draw it down slowly. "Show me."

"I'm definitely not the wisest man. But I'm fairly sure flashing you at your brother's engagement party is a bad idea."

I blink down at my hand resting on the zipper, knuckles pressed against a warm, bulging lump—

I jerk my hand back and turn my heated face toward the ink on his chest. "I meant, show me the scar on your thigh."

Mort's heavy sigh produces a familiar ache. "I'm sorry for springing that 'Hey' on you."

"Felix!" My brother calls.

Mort buttons his shirt, eyes never straying from mine.

Roch squashes me against his side. "First to find Mort, as always."

I can't find my voice.

Roch drops his arm and gestures Mort to follow him.

"Pineapple boxers, classy. Lauren spotted you and wants to chat."

Mort zips up, looking at me apologetically. "I'll be right back. We'll talk." He jostles after Roch.

The crowd swallows them as panic blasts through me.

I prop myself against the house and focus on the cool slats against my arm. The lavender tickling my shins. The Latin music combing over me on the breeze . . .

My breathing comes out in awkward chunks.

Mort is back.

It feels . . . too little, too late.

It feels . . . like all my wishes coming true.

A dozen memories assault me. Under simmering anger, I feel vulnerable and dizzy. I thought I was done with these feelings.

Mort engulfs Lauren in a full-bodied hug.

Maybe I'm not as done as I thought.

As I should be.

Chapter Four

MORT

"You're quiet and apologetic." Lauren cups my cheek, pinning me with dark eyes void of their usual music. "Figuring out how to make things right?"

Figuring out how to keep my wits despite Felix's gaze rampaging every inch of me.

I'm not immune. Not in the slightest. Not before I left, and not now.

But I try to be. *Try and mostly fail . . .*

"Yeah," I murmur.

I peer over Roch's shoulder. Felix stares into space, frowning. His dark hair sweeps over one eyebrow, and he tugs on his bright bow tie like it's choking him.

His gaze meets mine momentarily before he jerks his focus away and breezes directly toward the bridge.

I need to talk to him.

Lauren clears her throat and I give her an apologetic grimace.

"Don't hurt Roch again," she says, brushing past me into the arms of her florist cousin.

Roch folds his arms like he's unsure what will happen next. I don't want him to retreat. Not when he's given me this chance.

I step toward him and he rocks backward, cutting off Felix's path.

Roch swivels a relieved gaze on his brother. "Felix. Mort's all yours."

Felix's body twitches like he wants to veer around Roch and keep going. He focuses on the bridge and the bushes glowing in the setting sun. "I need to check on the twins."

"Where are they?"

"The cave."

It'd be quicker to walk through the park than trek over the hill. The excuse is obvious to me, and judging by Roch's quivering frown, it's obvious to Roch, too.

Felix breaks into a jog over the bridge.

My stomach cinches.

Roch murmurs, "Guess he's not as happy to see you as I thought he'd be."

I can fix this. Pray to God I can.

I chase after Felix.

The bridge groans underfoot. Tall trees and waist-high shrubs swallow me, muffling the chatter from the party. Felix is a dozen paces ahead on a steep incline. Dappled light glows over his flexing calves and green Chucks—bright green like the new foliage that piggybacks old bark all around us. "Felix, hold up a sec."

His back tenses before he plows up the fern-fringed dirt path.

We crest the hill and wind down a soggy track. Twice, Felix

glances at me over his shoulder. The looks are quick, but his expression flickers with relief that I'm following.

The third time he looks, he stumbles over a tree root with an *oof.*

I close half the distance between us. "You okay?"

He dusts himself off, snorting. "Your fault. Distracting me."

"Can we talk about that?"

He strokes his hand through dense Rangiora leaves, murmuring, "Where to start?"

"With my tactless entrance?"

Hollow laughter bursts from him. I wish I could see his face. "How about your tactless exit?"

"Yes, it—"

"How about that last 'later' you sent me?" His deep Pacific blue eyes flash to mine, beautiful and brimming with hurt. "*Later* usually implies a few hours. Not strolling back into our lives after twelve months and three days." He attempts another laugh, but it cracks. "And a *message*? Classy."

"I couldn't say it."

"Goodbye? Were you on the lam? Held at gunpoint? Immobilized in hospital?"

No, that was the Rochester family.

I close my eyes briefly. "I didn't want to say goodbye . . . I didn't want there to be one."

"You walked out of our lives."

"I regret not staying every day."

Felix turns and swats his eyes. He pushes through foliage, following the burbling stream.

He halts at a tree stump outside the glowworm cave. A cool breeze tunnels us with soft fingers, carrying April and May's hushed voices.

"I swear, Felix, if I could go back . . ."

His gaze rivets to the cave entrance.

I rub my nape, tipping my cap off. It lands between our feet and I leave it there. "I wrote messages every day. But I couldn't send them."

"Sometimes I'd see those three dots jumping on my screen. I'd wait hours, staring at our group chat." Felix chuckles to himself like he's admitted something stupid. It's not. God. His voice lifts, uncertainly. "You're really back?"

"To stay."

"What changed your mind about . . . wanting us?"

"I always wanted you." Felix blinks rapidly, long lashes damp. His pain is deeper than I ever guessed. It guts me. I want to crush him into a protective hug and promise never to hurt him again. "My dad was never there, but your mum . . . God. Do you know how many times I wanted to call her Mum, too? Dolores meant everything to me."

"You left before we went to hospital."

"She needed her kids around. Not . . . I respected her wishes."

"Her *wishes*? What kind of excuse is that?"

Felix scoops up my cap and settles it on his head.

I squeeze his shoulder and a shiver rolls through him. "There are no excuses," I say quietly. "I should've stayed. I fucked up."

"I have to get the twins. Get back to the party."

I pinch the cap and turn his face to mine. He's taller than Roch by an inch and his gaze levels at my nose. I swoop to meet his furiously blinking eyes.

Ah, Felix. "I don't ever again want to miss you like I have missed you. Not for a single second."

A sob wracks his body and he pushes away from me.

I'm right behind him. "Felix, please."

Felix trips over a protruding root. I catch him before he spears himself, and his back smacks against my chest. "Whoa."

April appears in the cave entrance, shrieking, "Don't impale your last kidney, stupid."

Felix slithers out of my slackening grip.

His last—what? Panic boils in my belly. I stare at the dirt-ruffled April, determined to have misheard. "What?"

Felix shakes his head, begging me to just *leave*, please.

Utilizing every ounce of my self-control, I wrench myself back down the path.

His last kidney?

I hear Felix's earlier words. *You left before we went to hospital.*

Before *we* went to hospital.

He wasn't just visiting his mum. He was in surgery alongside her.

The truth is an agonizing punch to my gut.

Behind me, Felix lures his sisters away from the cave. His chipper tone is forced, and it makes my throat ache. He banters with his sisters while gently admonishing them for lying about coming here.

The twins' voices melt into the distance.

Before I turn a bend, I notice my cap on Felix's head.

How can I *ever* make it up to him?

Chapter Five

MORT

Aching, frustrated, angry, I hunt the party for Felix's mum.

Barbecue-smoked breezes shiver over me, sinking through the buttonless gap of my shirt. Felix darts into the house. He doesn't look at me, but his stiff shoulders say he knows I'm there.

Roch's quizzical gaze hits mine, but Lauren kisses him and we're forgotten.

I pivot to find Tiffany glaring at me across the dance floor.

So much pain I have to repair. I raise a hand but she becomes a blur of fleeing gold.

I sigh. Fuck. Tomorrow. I'll talk to the girls tomorrow. First Dolores.

I stride around tables.

I shove off my footwear and step inside, right into the

kitchen; the air tastes of warm potpourri and cinnamon, achingly familiar, and I hurry through it.

I bypass the spiral staircase leading to Roch and Felix's floor, and head toward her bedroom. The open door leaks musky darkness into the hall. I take a breath, knock, and push inside.

The floor sticks under my clammy feet.

A lump stirs on the bed. Dolores speaks, voice muffled. "Is it time for the party?" She sits up and dabs her eyes. Her graying hair nests around her pale head. She freezes. "Oh. Mort."

The disappointment is palpable. "Dolores."

"You're back in town?"

"For good."

She smiles tightly, a mother guarding her young. "You've heard the wonderful news? Roch's engaged."

The subtext makes me want to laugh. Makes me want to fucking cry.

I flick on the light, and she flinches.

"With Lauren!" she continues. "Such a lovely woman."

"I'd say you must be happy, Dolores, but I'm not sure about that." I look toward the drawn curtains and the muffled sounds of jazz from the back yard, where Roch and Lauren are surely dancing the foxtrot.

Dolores picks up a glass of water from her nightstand, where it sits next to a leather bible. "Why are you here?"

"You told me you got an anonymous donor."

"I knew you'd stay if I told you the truth."

My jaw aches, but not as much as my heart. "I should have stayed regardless."

"I didn't want you to."

"Do you still feel so strongly about me?"

She looks away from me. "It's complicated."

"You were like a mum growing up. The hugs, the laughter,

taking me to soccer, feeding me dinner. You once loved me. I never changed. You might have only figured it out last year, but I was always gay. Yes, I loved your son, but he didn't love me back. Hell, that crush was five years ago. He's about to marry a 'lovely woman'. What's to be scared of?"

Her voice is quiet but carries crisply across the room. "He's not my only son."

"Felix?" I want to sound outraged, but I struggle pitching the lie. "I haven't looked at Felix that way."

"Maybe *you* haven't."

I swallow, feeling the ghost of Felix's earlier welcome tickling at my chest, at my zipper. I see him outside the cave, the hurt and anger in his eyes, the welled emotion.

Impervious Felix, broken.

A bitter thought hits me. "Your kids think I knew Felix donated his kidney and didn't care to be here." My voice strains. "Oh, God. Dolores." I love this woman so much. Even though she asked me to leave.

I loved her enough to do it.

The worst decision. The worst decision I've ever made.

"I won't let you cast me out again. This is my family too."

She buries her face in her hands. "It's complicated, Mort."

I hunker next to her on the soft bed and stroke her hair. Dark rings crease her eyes.

I have no words, and neither does she. I help her up and send her into the shower. I make her bed and lay out a blue dress the exact shade of her eyes. And Felix's.

When she emerges into the kitchen, I pass her a mug of freshly brewed coffee. Makeup masks her sad lines. A lock of hair has escaped; I tuck it into place while she drinks.

"There. Beautiful."

She sets her mug down, gnawing her lip as she stares out the window toward the pavilion.

"Your kids will be happy you're there," I murmur.

"I will be too." She looks guiltily over her shoulder at me. "Mort, it shouldn't feel complicated, but it does. When you stare at death, you not yourself anymore. I . . ."

I shake my head sadly. "Tonight, dance. Tomorrow, tell them the truth."

Chapter Six

FELIX

I'm a canvas of shivery goosebumps, and it has zero to do with being cold.

Stashed beside the family china cabinet, behind the parted door that leads from the dining room to the kitchen, I watch Mum heel toward the party. The back door bangs behind her like an exclamation mark to everything I just overheard.

Which is everything.

Stepping out of the bathroom, I'd halted at Mort's voice. Their traded lines were a blow to the gut. I stashed myself here when Mort ushered Mum to the shower, and I'm still here, staring through the gap into the kitchen. Trying to process it all.

Mort slouches against the counter, back to the windows overlooking the party, and scrubs his face with a groan. "Fuck," he utters softly. "God, Felix . . ."

His guilt and anguish engulf me. I quietly suck in coffee-laced air.

I'm tempted to step out and face him. Tempted to lean against his broad damp chest and grind my forehead against the warm crook of his neck until these uneasy feelings settle.

Tempted to tell him all is forgiven, and can't we go back to the way things were?

The teasing conversations. The generous laughter. The tight friendship. The . . .

The front door snaps as Mort leaves.

The sound propels me up the spiral staircase to my room.

My jitters compound with every raced step.

THE LAST GUEST LEAVES AT THREE IN THE MORNING.

The twins and Mum are long in bed, and Roch, Lauren, Tiffany and I are on cleanup.

I drop dishes into a soapy sink, splashing my front. "Dammit."

"Felix?"

Tiffany resisted bedtime to help clean. "You holding on there, Tiff?"

"Are *you*?"

I grin at her. "Of course."

"Right. Because a smile a day keeps thoughts of Mort away?"

It takes effort to hold my lips in place. "Mort, who?"

She sighs, twisting a vase of roses on the kitchen island.

"How'd you know I was thinking about him?"

Her eyes glisten as she sniffs a rose. "Because I am too."

I drop the plate I'm scrubbing and squeeze her into a hug, her hair tickling my nose.

She whispers, "How much do we hate him for coming back?"

Hate? I don't know. A little. A lot. Never. "He's . . . remorseful."

"Hmpf." She pulls back, eyeing the piles of dishes. "You keep washing and I'll dry?"

"Only if we change the conversation."

"Agreed." She stares at the drying rack, blushing. "Did you really mean it? About teaching me to drive?"

Was the pro side of her *Should I Learn to Drive* list growing? "You want to learn?"

She bites her lip. "Yes. No. Really not. Maybe?"

"Damn this suspension."

"Not meant to be then. Moving on."

I nudge her with my elbow. "Hang on, hang on. I'll quiz you on your theory. Or do you have a con list for theoretical driving too?"

She flicks soapy suds at me. I swat them off my nose with a laugh, chucking the dishtowel at her.

Lauren gracefully shuttles flute glasses inside, smiling at us, and Mum's "lovely woman" comment slams into my head. The rest of that conversation follows.

I scrub the china, busying myself until Roch relieves Tiffany and sends her to bed.

When it's just the two of us in the kitchen—Lauren resting in the lounge—Roch hip-checks me.

"Tonight's party—perfect. The music, the food, the pavilion . . . my soon-to-be wife. I need someone to slap me over the head to make sure I'm not dreaming. I swear, if the wedding is anything close to this, it'll be the best wedding I've been to."

"How many weddings have you been to?"

Roch huffs a laugh. "Snarky. Also, fair point."

"It'll be beautiful, Roch. I'm happy for you."

"I might believe you if you'd look at me." Roch takes the scrubbing brush hostage. "Plan to tell me what's up?"

"What do you mean?"

"You disappeared all evening, then returned to the party with a tight smile and red eyes." Roch holds my gaze affectionately. "Talk to me, Felix. You are the best brother in the entire world, and I hate seeing you down."

I slump against the counter, and Roch mirrors me.

"It's about Mum."

Roch grimaces. "Let me guess, the fact she doesn't drive anymore is driving—haha—you insane?"

I groan. "Losing my license hasn't exactly alleviated that stress. But no, it's not that."

"What's going on?"

"She doesn't"—I ball my hands at my sides—"like that Mort's gay."

"What?"

"He was like family and she asked him to leave. That's why he left us, Roch. Because she told him, and he listened. He stupidly listened."

All evening, I've fought not to let that conversation get the better of me. But it's no use. I turn to Roch and throw my arms around his neck. I need him to brother me right now.

Roch pats my back and coos. His voice is frayed with shock. "I don't—I can't believe it."

"He didn't know I was Mum's donor."

"You sound relieved at that."

I nod against his neck. It doesn't absolve Mort, but it eases the hurt. Fluttering behind my ribcage is an ugly, selfish hope that he would have changed his mind if he'd known the truth. That he'd have stayed for me.

But blaming Mort for my hurt isn't fair. If I'd been more outspoken about being Mum's donor . . . If I hadn't stayed quiet about it . . .

He was supposed to have known anyway.

I'd thought Mum had told him that last day, when he emerged from her bedroom with swollen eyes. When he dropped his cap low and slumped out the front door. Out of our lives.

I shudder.

"Oh, Felix, I'm sorry."

I pull out of Roch's embrace. "Me too."

I'm sorry Mum hurt Mort.

I'm sorry Mort felt compelled to leave.

I'm sorry for the way my thoughts mutate—how hard it is to look at Roch without seeing Mort. Mort gazing at Roch with a soft, halfway smile. Mort stepping in front of Roch when some dick made fun of him for ballroom dancing.

Mort alone in The Groove after Roch didn't return his feelings, head slammed against the headrest, throat bulging on a hard swallow as "Yesterday" blared from the radio.

I smile and fondly slap Roch over the head.

"What was that for?"

"Proving tonight isn't a dream."

Proving it really, really isn't. Even if I wish it were.

Chapter Seven

FELIX

A distant giggle stirs me out of my slumber and I inhale sleep-musty air. Floorboards creak outside my bedroom door.

Drowsily, I flick my covers off. If the twins think they're secretly draping a glowworm crown over me, they're in for a fright. A real good one, if I can manage it.

We'll laugh about it later—what a wonderful start to the day.

The door jiggles and swings open.

I leap into the doorway. "Away with your larvae—"

My growl cleaves into a shriek. Not April and May in matching pajamas, carrying a jar of worms.

Still hunched, I stare at the familiar tight landscape of Mort's chest under his safari shirt.

I straighten until I'm face to face with his startled amusement.

I scramble back, heat rushing to my cheeks.

He ogles me in the dusky hall light. "You look *mort*ified."

Somewhere in my belly there's a laugh, but it's numbed under my frazzled nerves. "What are you doing here?"

Mort steps into the room like he's done a thousand times before. Unlike those thousand times, his fingers are snapping open the button of his jeans. "We got off on the wrong foot."

"So you're . . . showing me your third one? In the middle of the night?"

Mort pauses at the zipper and rocks out a laugh. He walks to my blinds and yanks them open, letting an overcast morning sift gray light into my attic-slanted bedroom. It streaks over his blond hair and unshaven cheeks, emphasizing his chin dimple.

"It's almost nine."

"I was finally in deep sleep. Or maybe I'm still asleep, and this is a dream."

"Dream or nightmare?"

"Ha. I don't know."

Eyes twinkling, he takes my elbow and pulls me toward the window light.

I stumble against him, chest to chest, and my *oof* combs the underside of his jaw.

Mort grins and his hands work between us, air lapping against me as he shoves his pants to his knees. The back of his hand bumps my crotch, producing a shivery tingle.

Mort plants my fingertips over smooth, shiny skin that sits like an island among the light hairs on his legs. My gaze flies to his.

"Not an apparition, see?"

See, hear, smell, *and* feel. I trace the long scar that curves to his inner thigh. He twitches.

I remember that day in the bush. Mort's grunt as his army knife slipped off the wet wood he was whittling and plunged into his thigh. The blood welling through his shorts, his large hands too shaky to staunch the wound; my hands clamping his thigh, yelling for Roch to find help. My frantic pleas for him to be okay, and Mort's rumbling voice in my ear assuring me he'd be fine.

I tighten my hand over his scar, feeling his pulse jump warmly. "Why are you here?"

His gaze drops to my waist. His voice comes out a raspy plea. "Show me yours?"

I pull away, folding my arms tightly. "It's just a scar."

"It's not 'just' anything."

Touching Mort screws with my synapses. I can't *think.*

From downstairs, April yells, "Felix! Pack our bag?"

"Soccer!" I thank the stars for the reprieve and hurtle to my dresser.

Mort chuckles. "Roch messaged this morning about their game. I'm here to drive you guys there. And everywhere else the next six months."

"Say, what?"

"Consider me your chauffeur."

Did Roch put Mort up to this? He's overly optimistic, believing I can endure the next six months with Mort driving me places.

Driving me insane, is what'll happen.

"Unnecessary," I say, and yank out clothes. "Jason is helping today. Every other day there's a bus."

"Jason? You mean Jace and Coop, right?"

"They're not back from opal hunting in Australia yet. Jason is a guy I met at work." I notice Mort's red cap that I'd stuffed alongside my bow ties. "He visits the home multiple times a week to read to his granddad."

"Jason," he murmurs as if tasting bitterness. "Are you close?"

"Don't have time for friends, so I suppose that makes Jason an awesome guy who's going out of his way to help me."

Mort is quiet and I force myself not to glance over my

shoulder. He clears his throat. "Next time you need a lift, then. I'm better than the bus."

His footsteps creak over floorboards and groan down the spiral staircase.

Relief slides through me. *Get a grip, Felix.* He's Roch's best friend. He's probably trying to make amends for Roch—the guy he's likely still in love with. I'm an obstacle to their happy reunion.

I draw in a steadying breath and scramble into my clothes.

Time to concentrate on the important things. Like Mum and my sisters. Like transporting April and May to their soccer game.

Downstairs, I grab our sorry-looking sports bag by its threadbare handles and dive into the supply cupboard. Soccer boots, shin pads, practice ball. Check, check, check.

April and May are already dressed and snapping bow ties around their sport's collars. I blink at them from their bedroom doorway. "Erm, it's a soccer game, girls."

"Who says we can't kick balls in style?"

Their red bow ties match the uniform stripes. Tenderness creeps up my chest. *Is this how Roch felt when I started copying him?*

It's painful how hard I tried to mimic Roch growing up, right down to his tie and shoes. For a while we could have been twins, if not for my weird blue eyes.

I glance from the girls to my outfit.

Only since finishing high school had I taken the bow tie and made it my own, opting for bright colors and pairing it with casual jeans and sneakers.

I like my look, and I'm sticking with it. But it sends heat to my cheeks, wondering how much I copied Roch because I wanted his best friend's attention.

I pack the girls' mouth guards. "Two minutes. Get your Groove on."

My phone buzzes. Jason, probably, to tell me he's on his way.

I race to the kitchen. Mort stands at the spluttering percolator that steams with mouthwatering coffee.

My socks skid over the tile and I catch myself on the counter. "You're still here!"

"Feel free to feel me up again to be sure."

I grab bottles, snorting. His lopsided grin has my lips tugging up on their own, and—

No. Not ready to sink into that level of comfort with him again.

I focus on filling the bottles and searching the pantry for snacks.

Mort's voice does sneaky things to my chest. "I thought about cleaning up from the party, but looks like you saw to it already."

"Roch, Lauren, and Tiffany helped."

"How is Tiffany?"

"You haven't spoken to her yet?"

"Unfortunately not."

"She's probably sleeping."

"She's awake. Just avoiding me."

I grumble, "Maybe I should get some tips."

Mort laughs, filling two mugs with coffee.

I drop the packed sports bag and pluck a fuchsia rose from a bouquet. It's not dance class—or a certain person she's crushing on—but maybe it'll lighten Tiffany's day. I turn to race into the hall but Mort, the sneaky bastard, blocks my path, offering coffee.

I pinch the stalk, and the rose bows toward him.

His brow arches. "For me?"

"Not this time." I eye the mug, and I'm slammed back to yesterday. How tenderly Mort tucked Mum's hair into place as she drank his coffee. "I'm . . . I'm not thirsty."

I sidle past him and bowl into Mum on her way to the bathroom. “Sorry.”

“Morning, Felix.” She pinches my cheeks. “My, you look rosy today.”

I pray to the heavens Mort isn’t overhearing.

“Suits you.” She shuffles away, and I lurch my embarrassed ass to Tiffany’s room.

I shut her door and lean against her con-heavy driver’s license list. “Craaaaap.”

Tiffany’s head shoots up from behind her phone, where she’s nestled in her armchair. “You look flushed.”

I pin her with a scowl. Her soft, tinkering laugh makes the mortification worth it.

I pass her the flower and notice a practice driver’s test on her phone. “You know, I’ll find a way for you to learn.”

She takes a long lungful of rose, cheeks pinking. “I don’t want to. This is just theory.”

“My, Tiffany, you look positively *flushed* . . .” She scowls as I back out her room with a knowing smirk.

I race upstairs, throw on a trench coat and some shoes, and stuff my pockets with bits and bobs before braving the kitchen again.

I act like Mort isn’t sitting there, sipping coffee, leaning against the sink, watching me. I grab my keys and yank the bag—

The handle snaps off and the bag thuds to the floor. I scoop the darn thing, hike it through a cold-ass drizzle, and dump it into the trunk of the station wagon.

My phone buzzes. Water drops plop on the screen as I read the messages.

Jason: Super sorry, can’t make it. Grandad slipped and he needs me. :/

Roch: You guys good? Mort show up? Wishing the girls an awesome game. Xx

I slouch against the wagon, brainstorming a solution. There isn't one, though. I reluctantly slip inside and walk up to Mort, who's still standing against the counter with his old favorite mug displaying the chemical formula of caffeine.

"Everything okay?" he asks.

I groan and juice my keys.

He studies me over the rim of his mug, then pushes off the counter like he can read what I'm planning to ask. Hell, he's already nodding.

"Wait."

He lifts his brow.

I need to set boundaries around this. Us. Whatever. "Driving us around doesn't automatically mean we'll be friends."

He nods. Regret paints his expression. "We'll be whatever you want us to be."

"Well that's . . . that's"—a shiver twirls in my belly and I swallow—"something."

He motions toward the keys I'm furiously flipping over my finger. "Shall I start as your chauffeur?"

I clench the keys into a fist. "You have to get the twins on your side again, too."

"Part of my day plan."

"Don't think it'll be easy. It's April and May—you left them with go-kart designs and no help to make them."

"They still want to build go-karts?"

"Yes, but I doubt with you."

Mort claps his hands together. "Let me work on removing that doubt."

He ushers me out into the nasty, sleety cold, urging April and May to hurry. We clomp over the brick path, dewy grass slick on my Chucks and Mort's boots.

"Where's the game?"

"Hutt, this week. Karori, next. Driving us won't be an easy job."

"I hope not. I want to spend as much time with you as I can."

A breathy squeak escapes my mouth, and I stop at The Groove's hood. "I can catch a bus to and from work and haul groceries on foot. It's only soccer and dance classes we need rides to. Maybe not so hard after all? Jesus it's cold, why are we standing here?"

Mort's warm fingers curve around mine. "Gah."

He carefully peels back my fingers. "Can't drive without the keys."

Mort plucks them from my clammy palm and heads to the driver's side.

I shake off the tickle his touch leaves behind. "Easy on the clutch and avoid top gear."

Mort shoots a bemused look over the roof of the car. "You forget. I taught you to drive in The Groove."

Nope, not forgotten. Not one gear-shifting moment.

The passenger door opens and Mort pulls back into his seat with a wink that makes my throat dry. "Coming?"

"I wish."

"Sorry?"

I wince. "Nothing."

April and May jostle past me and dive into the back seat. They notice Mort in the front and side-eye each other with a slight grimace. Mort has no clue what he's in for.

I hesitate between the two open doors.

My nerves seriously can't handle being this close to Mort.

I dive into the back seat, propelling May into the middle.

Mort glances at me in the rearview mirror as I shut the door, then nods. "Going for the full chauffeur experience. Okay."

"Wait." May jerks a finger. "Who's shutting the passenger door?"

Mort starts the engine and smirks at May in the mirror. "I'll get that."

"How?"

Mort hits the gas, peeling from the curb. The door slams. "Physics."

Physics?

We're standing at the side of a soggy soccer field, bracing against the wind chill. It's the first half of the game, and April and May are hurtling up and down the pitch, dominating the ball. I've barely looked at Mort since his frustratingly impressive win with the twins.

One word, and they forgave him. Just like that.

The girls make it seem easy, whereas every second I'm battling memories and impulses to . . . to . . . Jesus, I don't even know.

Mort shifts, bumping the length of his arm against mine. "What are you scowling at?"

I peer at him out the corner of my eye. "*Physics?*" My tone is all bafflement and awe.

"I also left a science mystery kit in your living room."

I sigh. "You sure know what turns their gears."

Mort nods. "I take greasing seriously."

I shake my head. "Well played and perfectly pitched—down to the spark in your eye as you said it. So slick, so simple, so effective."

I fold my arms and concentrate on April dribbling the ball toward the goal. She narrowly misses a shot. May gives her a high-five anyway before racing downfield.

I side-eye Mort, who cheers them on.

He catches me and I avert my gaze, clearing my throat. "Greasing won't work on me."

"It worked once."

Nope, I'd recall otherwise. "Jog my memory."

His shoulder bumps mine, and his words skitter around my ear. "You were upset, and I greased you until you weren't upset anymore."

I roll my eyes. "That has never happened."

"Sure it has. You laughed and everything."

"You're making this up."

"Mmm, am I?"

I bounce out a laugh, twisting to face him. "Yes!"

His gaze flitters to my upturned lips and he dons a soft expression. "I don't think I am."

The ref blows the whistle for half time.

After a team huddle, April and May jog over to us. Their practice ball nestles in a dip of grassy earth a few yards away.

I grab their water bottles, mumbling dissatisfaction as the twins fist-bump Mort.

Mort chuckles under his breath and gives the twins some tips. "Ball control is good. Endurance, too. Keep your heads up though. Spatial awareness on the field is key."

"You've got to coach us again," April pleads.

Mort hunches to their level. "We'll work around your dance classes."

"We quit dance."

Mort gives a furrowed nod. His gaze flickers my way. *What else has changed?*

Everything, Mort.

Everything and nothing.

He squeezes their shoulders. "Tell me all about it this afternoon?"

"What's this afternoon?"

"Go-kart plans that need attention. The junk yard."

He's such a teacher. Always thinking up creative, hands-on ways to educate. I don't know where he mines his vibrant energy.

Maybe it's all that coffee he drinks at our place.

April says something that has Mort playfully tugging on her braid, smirking.

My chest squeezes. I tip my head up into a swirling breeze and the cool air combs my face.

He only strolled back into our lives yesterday. I can't have forgiven him that fast.

The twins crowd me for water and snacks. I hand them muesli bars and salted nuts. May's braid has come undone—hair tie snapped—and I dig around my pockets for a spare one.

"You got tissues?" April asks.

I hand her some.

"My sock has a hole in the toe," May complains. I have an emergency pair.

"One side of my shoelace snapped, too."

I'm prepared for it all.

"Heel skin?" April asks. I pull four Band-Aids out. "Get this to May before she puts that sock on."

April slinks to May sitting on the grass, shaking out her replacement sock.

I catch Mort eyeing my pockets with a bewildered blink. "What's next? A rabbit?"

I reach into my deepest pocket and wedge out his cap. I pull it on Mort's head. "There."

My gaze latches on to his. My fingers freeze at the rim of his hat.

I drop my hands and rock back on my heels. Mort tugs at my lapels, keeping me in place. He inspects my heavy-duty cotton trench coat. His hands slide inside, knuckles grazing my chest as he feels for the inner pockets.

I suck in a breath and urge my voice to stay in control, but he must feel the vibrations of my pounding heart. "What are you doing?"

"My job."

"Your job is feeling me up?"

"My job is science. Investigating curious phenomena and making sense of limitless pockets."

"Your job is very hands on."

"I don't mind getting handsy in the pursuit of knowledge."

"You didn't see me stuffing my pockets at the wagon?"

"I thought you grabbed water bottles and the ball, not . . . your entire supply cupboard."

My stomach chooses that moment to rebel at my breakfast-less departure.

Mort's gaze hits mine with a twinkle. "Anything for *you* in these pockets? Snack maybe?"

His fingers skate over my stomach and it lurches again. Possibly not entirely hunger-related. It skitters through me like a breathless kind of tickle.

I gesture to the twins wolfing down their muesli bars. "As much as I wish my pockets were limitless, that was the last of the food."

Mort reaches into his jacket pocket, fishes around, and triumphantly pulls out a bitesize Moro bar. He unwraps the chocolate and presses it against my lips. "Eat up."

"Is this you greasing me?" I murmur, lips butting against the blunt end of the bar.

"Only if it's working."

His eyes crinkle at the edges and his mouth quirks in that lazy half-smile. *Oh, crap. Crap. Crap.* "Not in the slightest."

"Let me chew on that, while you chew on this."

He nudges the bar past my lips and takes advantage of my chuckle to force it into my mouth. Caramel-goodness bursts over my tongue just as the second half starts.

Mort immerses himself in the game, cheering from the sidelines, scrolling up and down the flank alongside the girls.

When the final whistle blows, Mort claps the loudest, encouraging them for the good game, even if they lost.

He chucks a casual arm around my shoulders as the girls shake hands with the other team.

"They've always idolized you," I say. I keep my eye on the field. "They love science because you're passionate about it. They love soccer because they want to be "jocky geeks" just like you." I look at him. "I shouldn't be surprised you won them over so easy."

Mort steers his tender expression to the twins running toward us, their bow ties bouncing.

"What will it take to win *you* over?"

"I . . ." I slam my mouth shut. "Keep greasing, and you'll find out."

Chapter Eight

MORT

Keep greasing, and you'll find out.

I'm taking that line as gospel, and it's the reason I'm resting against the side of The Groove Monday morning; sun warms my nape and shoulders, stretching toward the Rochester house.

Harried yells leaking from inside tell me it's Go Time. The girls and Felix will emerge any second for school and work. They think they're catching the bus. Not if I can help it.

Tiffany bursts outside first. Stuffing her white shirt into her blue pleated skirt, she drapes her uniform blazer over her arm.

My stomach feels heavy as I step toward her. She pauses at the gate, and I halt.

"Care for a ride to school?"

She glares at me and shakes her head. "I'm good with the bus."

She kicks down the street, and I rub my jaw. I teach ten to thirteen year olds; I'm not equipped for navigating the emotions of sixteen-year-old girls. Especially if they're pissed at me.

I suppose she needs more time to adjust to me being around.

I guess all I can do is keep trying.

"Mort!" April flies toward me, her backpack bouncing behind her thick braids. "Are you chauffeuring us again?"

"Like yesterday to the beach. Like the day before to soccer. Like every day for the foreseeable future." *I hope.*

I open the back door for her, and she giggles and slides in. May follows in matching braids.

The twins might play soccer and love science like me, but their style and quick wit is all Felix. The mix jerks my insides around.

I *need* this family in my life.

I shut the back door, hoping this will encourage Felix to take the front seat.

Felix trots from the house but stalls halfway when he spots me.

He's wearing a dark blue shirt, white bow tie, with a brown-leather shoulder bag that falls to his hip. He looks smart and casual all at once. He looks perfect.

I'm here to repair my family. Not indulge in an attraction that could mess up my relationship with Roch, with his mum, with the girls.

Yet, I keep indulging.

I can't damn well help it. There's something about Felix that curls warmly under my skin and begs me closer.

Friendship and family. That's what I need to focus on.

Or perhaps I should focus on what I'll have if things don't work out: no one.

Just an achingly empty house that continues to smell like a dad who never cared.

Felix eyes me warily, then regains his composure and continues to The Groove. "Okay, so a teacher, a man with an honors degree in physics and chemistry, a—let's call him a smart man—would have understood that I meant it when I said we'd catch the bus."

I cross my arms. "Sounds like a clever guy. Pity what you got is a past friend, who spent half the night searching for his old car key, so he could surprise you this morning by giving you and the girls a ride."

Felix glances through the back window, fiddling with the bronze latch of his bag. "Tiffany's not—"

"He's also a man who is rendered useless at a teenage girl's glare."

Humor twitches Felix's cheek. "Cream of the crop."

I tip my cap. "At your service."

Felix steps toward the back and I slide an inch over the door handle. He halts a breath from me, his gaze shooting to mine. "You convince me to let you drive us but then you block my way into the car. I'm questioning those degrees you have."

"You should. I've forgotten everything I learned at uni."

Felix blinks toward the passenger door. The tentative humor edging his eyes fades. He gulps and rocks on his heels.

He fiddles more with his bag the nearer he is to me. I suspect he wouldn't entirely hate sitting in the front.

"I . . . I'll spell it out for you, then—"

I slide away before he can continue. I want him in the front —God, yeah—but only when he's ready. "Jump in, I'll take you anywhere you need to be."

Two weeks later, I'm really in The Groove. I transport the Rochesters from A to B and Z and beyond—as Felix likes to say—and transport myself to work. Kresley Intermediate is five minutes from Felix's job at the retirement home, so it makes sense.

After teaching, Felix and I begin the driving rounds. Most missions run smoothly, but driving Tiffany around proves uncomfortable; only the radio—or Felix—breaks the silence.

Like Felix is doing right now, at the end of my third week chauffeuring. But once he finishes doling out excited praise for Tiffany passing her driver's theory test, they settle into silence.

I wish I could strike up conversation with her. Wish I could find a way to reconnect.

A hard ball lumps in my throat.

When we arrive at the dance studio, she shoots out the wagon, swinging her dance bag toward the old brick building like she can't escape fast enough. I stifle a sigh and stare at the sun setting on the orange brick. Neon blue and green light up the adjoining arcade.

"Felix, you heading inside?" He always follows her in.

I swivel and inspect through the gap between the front seats.

Felix's eyes are closed, head resting against the window, mouth grimaced. Light crowns his unruly dark hair, streaking it with copper. Shadows from moving traffic dance across his face.

He's clearly exhausted.

Wake up, make breakfast, wrangle the girls to school, work eight hours. Chauffeur the girls to practice, run errands, bring kids home, make dinner, bathe the girls, read them a story. Fall into bed six hours away from his personalized version of Groundhog Day.

That is Felix's life.

He's particularly tired today, though, and a little flushed. Maybe he's coming down with a spring cold. The last thing this guy needs. The universe owes him a break.

Felix eyes me sleepily. "That's one wild frown."

I readjust my cap. "Tailored just for you."

His cheeks dimple. "What's the matter?"

"Are you in the mood to talk?"

Felix pushes himself upright, leaving a smear of condensation on the glass. "About what?"

"Everything."

He squints, hesitant. "Define everything."

"How's your mum doing?"

A whimper-laugh drizzles out of him. "I'd rather talk about the sorry state of my love life."

"How sorry are we talking?"

He stares at me blankly. "You first."

I laugh. "Remember when I dragged you for coffee at Zealandia Café and we bumped into my colleague Jack and—"

"And Ben McCormick. Trust me, a week is not long enough to erase the embarrassment of almost toppling into them."

"Jack's the guy I've been flirting with at work."

Felix gives me a standard cardboard smile. Those smiles are pissing me off. His days are littered with them.

I fight back a growl. "I'm fairly sure he's a lost cause."

"Considering his hand was wedged into Ben's back pocket, I'd say he is." Felix stares at passing cars. "Are you gutted?"

"He's a decent guy. Hot and charming but mostly just a distraction."

Felix whips his head toward me. "From what?"

I give him a pointed look.

"From missing us," he murmurs.

Yeah. From that tiny ache that's ripping me open.

"Do you miss us all equally?" Felix claps his mouth shut. "Forget it. That's like asking a parent who their favorite child is. No matter how untrue, they'll swear they don't have one."

I peer at him through the rearview mirror. "I missed you all equally."

"You'll make a good parent." He drops back in his seat and

catches my eye, mouth twisted toward a smile. A real one this time.

I want more of his smiles. I want Felix to see what we could have together. I want to graduate from "chauffeur" to Guy He Has Fun With.

Felix clears his throat and clicks his seatbelt open. "I should get inside."

"Tiffany has an hour left." I eye the arcade. "We can use it."

Felix hums. "Yeah, okay. We're out of parchment paper and detergent. The Warehouse is still open. We can swing by."

Parchment paper and detergent? That's how he wants to spend a free hour? Felix doesn't know how much he needs me. "Out of the car, sunshine."

"What?"

I unfold from the wagon to the pavement and brace an arm on the roof of the car to look at him. "Hop out, or I'm coming around and making a show of opening your door."

Chapter Nine

FELIX

I SCUTTLE OUT OF THE WAGON.

Mort locks up and leads us to the fast-food vendor in the arcade. A plate of steaming fries and two drinks later, we slide into the corner booth.

Mort folds up his shirtsleeves against the stuffy heat; his forearms glitter under the light. I'm glad that his cap shadows his eyes, but it also irritates me.

Glad, because it stops me from analyzing his every expression. Irritated, because I want to analyze his every expression.

He's been keeping personal space the last few weeks and avoiding underhanded tactics to lure me into the passenger seat.

I *want* to ride shotgun, but there's an unspoken understanding between Mort and me: the passenger seat is symbolic. If I sit in it, it's means we're friends again. And I'm not ready to announce that yet.

Mort catches me watching him. My chest is thoroughly whipped.

Heat simmers up my neck. I rub my nape as Mort drizzles hot sauce over the fries and nudges the plate toward me. "Eat."

I pinch a fry from the bottom. "Sick of driving us around yet?"

"It keeps me from being home and dwelling on the emptiness of my home life." His lips twist wryly.

I feel the ache under his rugged voice.

I pinch another fry. "Sounds like you need this chauffeur gig more than we do."

"It's a symbiotic relationship."

"Next time you need the twins on your side, 'symbiotic' is your free pass."

Mort leans back. The angle sheds light over his humored eyes.

He catches my hesitation and twirls a fry. "Go on, say what's on your mind."

I lower my voice. "I'm sorry. About your dad."

He chews and swallows—harder than a single fry warrants, in my opinion. "I'm sorry too, but not about my dad."

Oh.

Flustered, I tug another fry free.

"Why are you playing Jenga with the fries?"

I slouch back on the bench, mirroring him. "I'm not into spicy food."

Mort pulls his cap down and swears, giving the sauce-coated fries an anguished look. "Roch loves hot sauce. Habit, sorry."

Roch. Habit.

My eyes flit away to the clumps of kids framed by screens of dazzling neon light.

He's not over him. He'll never be over him, and I need to stop—

"So, are you, ah, keeping his house?" I croak.

Mort's brow crunches. He casts the fries aside. "I don't want a single object that was dad's. But at the moment, it's a place to crash and a vehicle to drive."

He curls a finger for me to follow him, which I do, blindly. I'd probably follow him to hell.

I keep my voice breezy. "With how much you drive The Groove—and I've seen you use it without us—you could probably sell your dad's car."

He glances over his shoulder. "You know what? I will."

"Really, Mort, I didn't think I had that much power over you."

Mort walks backward to the chip counter. "Don't let it go to your head. Or . . . do."

He orders more chips. "What do you want to do first?" he asks, sliding his wallet back.

You.

His brows rocket up as if he reads my mind.

"You decide."

He leads me to Dance Dance Revolution. "Think we can crack my old score?"

I lean against the bars bolted to the floor. "Since when has dancing ever been my thing?"

His gaze slinks to my feet. "Do you really hate it?"

"No other choice when you're born with two left feet."

"I like your two left feet."

I reluctantly slide onto the plate next to his. "It's true. Flattery gets you everything."

Mort's laugh startles a nearby teen into dropping his coins. Mort nudges my shoulder with his and speaks more softly and earnestly than my shot nerves can handle: "Prepare for endless flattery, then."

Crap.

I swallow hard. I can't handle tenderness from Mort. It stirs up . . . feelings. Impossible feelings that have no place to grow amidst Mort and Roch's epic friendship.

Feelings their shared smiles and secrets have trampled. Feelings they'll trample again when they reunite as best friends.

I push the flutters down.

"Actually, I think . . . I'll watch after all."

"Are you sure?"

My smile stings. "Yes."

Mort frowns. "You don't have to dance, Felix. Don't pretend to be happy for my benefit. Do whatever you need to be happy for *you.*"

My smile wavers, but I manage to hold it until Mort dances to *Always on My Mind.*

He braces the bar behind him; his forearms flex as he dances over the floor pads. His body is angled toward the ceiling, and when his hips thrust a third time, I have to look away.

When he's done, he winces. "Ouch. Nowhere near as good as I used to be."

He scrolls to past scores, and MORT and ROCH flash in first and second place. Their names side by side is the last jab to my gut I can handle.

I encourage Mort to try again, and I slink into Tiffany's dance class.

The spacious room is probably the size of the arcade. A floor-to-ceiling mirrored wall reflects three couples dancing a professional-grade samba. Lauren stands near the sound system, eyeing their moves.

If she notices me, she doesn't let on.

Tiffany notices, though. Her gaze flitters over me during a turn.

I stand at the windows and watch the dancers deliver the frantic steps with poise. Tiffany's fair skin contrasts beautifully with her partner Arjun's dark complexion.

Lauren stops the music, delivers notes to each couple, and

watches them dance again. She slides over and chats with me, since Roch's regretfully swamped at work.

When it's over, I sling Tiffany's sports bag over my shoulder and trundle into the foyer.

Tiffany plucks my sleeve. "Felix? You all right?"

"Um . . . yes."

"Um . . . I don't believe you." She stops, right beside the short tunnel to the arcade. "What has he done now?"

"Who?" I ask, but I know who she's talking about.

She gives me a bland look. "Only Mort gets underneath your fake smiles."

"Shh." I glance down the tunnel. "They're not fake." She rocks a disbelieving huff. "Not all the time."

Tiffany waves to Arjun as he leaves and I raise my hand belatedly.

"I get it, Felix. It's hard to be happy with Mum's ups and downs, with my mopey moods, with being stuck with April and May."

My gaze snicks back to Tiffany. "No, no, Tiff—"

"You need a life outside us."

"I have a life . . ."

Tiffany draws her bag off my arm and hoists it over her shoulder. "One week. Find a partner. I'm teaching you to dance."

She veers around me toward the exit. I lunge for her elbow. "Just a sec."

She turns back, waiting.

I whisper to be extra careful. "When will you talk to Mort again?"

She whispers back, "I do talk to him."

"More than one-word answers."

"Maybe when you've forgiven him."

"What makes you think I haven't?"

"Besides the frown you sported half my lesson?" She folds her arms. "You still ride in the back seat."

Wait a second. "Are you not speaking to him on *my* behalf?" My heart softly hiccups.

Having a sister as loyal as Tiffany makes every hardship worth every sad minute.

I *will* make her smile so hard one day.

"Show me you're truly happy with Mort around," she says, "and I'll be happy he is too."

She brushes a kiss on my cheek and slips outside to The Groove.

I stare after her, amazed yet overwhelmed at the challenge.

Mort calls my name, and I dash after Tiffany to the car.

On our way home, he doesn't ask why I disappeared or why I'm acting skittish.

And I don't tell him it's unbearable being in love with him.

Chapter Ten

MORT

I RUB THE STEERING WHEEL AND WATCH TIFFANY AND FELIX walk up the pathway. I wish I was with them. Wish I was welcomed into their brightly lit home full of love and laughter.

I haven't fixed things enough to hang out there nights. Yet. But I'm working on it.

In the meantime . . .

I sigh, and drive to my place.

The villa is dark and cold, and the walls creak. I head straight to my childhood bedroom and kick off my boots.

I distract myself by ordering parts for Felix's sisters' go-karts. Then I busy myself in a book.

But the distractions don't last. Every night is a reminder of how empty my life got when I left the Rochesters. It's a reminder how empty it will be again if I fuck this up.

And yet.

Every night, I ache with desire to be close to Felix. I

imagine us sharing a bed, his squirmy heat rubbing against my tight body . . .

I grab a pillow and yell into it.

I haven't even earned his friendship back yet.

Besides, I won't risk losing all the Rochesters by chancing an encounter with Felix.

So why, then, is it impossible not to flirt with him?

A WEEK AFTER OUR VISIT TO THE ARCADE, I'M IN THE BUSHES with April and May, hunting for fallen wood to repurpose into their go-karts.

We've found some long, flexible twigs for part of the frame, and the girls are currently distracted by a beehive.

I perch on a moss-covered tree stump. Wind rustles through foliage, and newly bloomed mushrooms whisper against my calves.

Hours we've studied the bush, and hours I've wondered how another Rochester is doing.

I draw out my phone and open a private chat with Felix.

Me: I'm imagining you in bed.

I'm lucky enough to get an immediate response.

Felix: Ha. Ha. Save flirting for someone who wants it.

I hum at that, and reply.

Me: How are you doing?

I attach a photo of the twins crowded over their go-kart designs.

Felix: Sick. I can't get anything done, but in the same breath, I'm bored. You guys look like you're having . . . an educational time.

I grin.

Me: What needs done?

Felix: Dinner. Pack the girls' sleepover bags for Nicole's. I'm asking Mum . . .

Dolores? Pulling through in his time of need? Unlikely.
My phone vibrates again.

Felix: I give up. Voice is barely working.

He's painting quite a sickly picture, and it's begging me to see it up close and personal.

Me: You know what will help you recover?

Felix: Distracting myself from my chest pain by getting RSI in my thumb from all this chatting with you?

Me: An outing.

Felix: You forget how debilitating the man-flu is. Getting out of bed is impossible.

I head to the girls, who are excitedly pointing out bees crawling around the tree trunk.

I take another picture and send it to Felix, then tell April and May it's time to head back.

Felix: Look at us. We both caught bugs.

He might be sick, but his cheek is sharp.

Me: The twins and I will come get you.

Felix: I haven't showered in three days. Last time I made it to the bathroom, I left my underwear puddled on the floor.

Me: Correction: I will come get you.

The girls race ahead and I stroll after them.

Felix: Seriously, no one wants to see a grown man crusted in snot.

Me: Like I give a damn how snot-crusted you are. I'm making dinner, getting the girls ready to be picked up, and then I'm taking you for some fresh air.

Three dots jump on screen, stop, and jump again.

The lengthy time it takes him to answer suggests he's editing his responses.

What are you thinking, Felix?

His message pops through.

Felix: I'll put underwear on.

"YOU'RE BUNDLING ME INTO THE BACK SEAT."

I'm belting Felix in, too, if I can ever find the buckle. The car light is busted.

His freshly brushed breath slides over my neck. "But . . . but . . ."

I wedge the buckle out from under his ass, causing him to gasp. It morphs into a small cough that puffs at my shirt collar.

Belt . . . in.

I pause in triumph. His features are shadowy in the night, but I'm close enough to make out details. Swollen nose and top lip, rugged scruff, wavy hair knotted behind one ear, and spare tissue stuffed into his shirt pocket.

My lips jump at Felix's half-hearted attempt at tying his bow tie.

He's wrecked, but wrecked suits him well.

He lolls his head back and shuts his eyes. "But I'm at my weakest. This was your opportunity to load me in the front and I wouldn't have had the energy to resist."

I laugh and crawl off him. "I thought your voice was barely working?"

I shut his door and slide into the driver's seat.

Felix attempts a glare, but he only pulls off a rumpled puppy.

"My voice *was* barely working until you plowed into my bedroom. Then it perked up."

"Perked up at the sight of me? I thought I was supposed to flatter you?"

Felix groans. "Imagine your arm hurting badly. That's me whacking you."

The hills are well and truly behind us before I let Felix hook my gaze in the rearview mirror. I like the awestruck looks he slants me like he can't help it.

Our eyes hold in the dark. Heat races through me.

Felix turns away first, like always, and like always, I miss it.

He's Roch's younger brother.

You want his friendship. Something guaranteed to last.

"Eyes on the road, Mort," he grumbles.

A flurry of frustrated laughter zips to my middle. I hold it in, driving toward the glittering city lights fringing the inky harbor.

"So for this outing," he says, frowning at the passing streets. "What do you have planned? Keep in mind I'm weak and pathetic, and if dinner's involved, I've suddenly developed an allergy to soup."

Ah, Felix. He knows how to pull at my grins.

A familiar sign flashes ahead. I know exactly where we're going.

I check the dashboard clock: twenty past eight. "I'm thinking greasy food. Good view. Great conversation."

I wink at him in the mirror. His mouths ticks up. "I'm thinking you're promising a lot."

Chapter Eleven

FELIX

Mort is not overpromising.

We have greasy McDonalds in our hands—cold milkshakes cradled between our thighs—and the 1989 classic *When Harry Met Sally* is about to play on a giant outdoor movie screen at the Wainui drive-in theatre.

Ten minutes into previews, Mort removes the headrest to better my view.

Not that I'm paying attention to the big screen. Mort's phone, on the other hand . . .

I shake my head at the contact's name I'm staring at. Their last chat must have been recent because it comes in third after my name and Roch's.

"Pax Polo?" Mort wears a lazy grin. "Your phone is kidding me."

"Is it?"

"You know *the* Pax Polo?"

Mort gulps his milkshake in a deliberate attempt to make me stew in suspense.

A deliberate attempt that's working.

He pops off his straw with a smack of his lips. "Pax and Cliff fostered a girl who was in my class. She was struggling so they asked for regular meetings. Regular meetings turned into the occasional dinner invite."

"You had 'occasional dinner invites' with my absolute favorite rock star of all time?"

"I thought the lead from Tepid Creek was your favorite rock star of all time."

"Aside from Pax Polo, yes." I stare at his phone again. Pax freaking Polo! "Lauren would go nuts. Finagle an autograph for Lauren and your Roch problems are solved."

"That easy, huh?"

"If you take greasing up as seriously as you claim to, it'll be your Holy Grail."

Mort rubs his jaw and laughs, but his eyes flash at the reminder he and Roch aren't what they once were.

I accidentally turn off Mort's screen. I reluctantly hand it back. "What is Pax Polo like?"

"In a word? Energetic."

I stare at him. "More words?"

Mort's laugh rumbles warmly. "He's an overeager puppy who's head-over-heels in love with his husband. Even when they snipe at each other, they can barely hold back their grins. And yet, their relationship is surprisingly tender."

"Is that the type of relationship you'd like?" It pops out without a second thought. I blame my cold and being delirious.

Deliriously in love.

I drown the truth with a couple of salty fries and a gulp of banana milkshake.

"Yeah, Felix. That's the kind of relationship I want."

"I'm sorry Roch didn't love you back."

Holy shit.

My cheeks burn and my grip is slipping on my oversized McDonalds cup.

I wish the audio soundtrack wasn't muted. Wish something would break the silence other than my raspy breaths.

It's not like Mort doesn't know I know. Hell, I followed him the day Roch broke his heart. Followed him to The Groove, where he sobbed damp tears against my nineteen-year-old shoulder. Where I rubbed trembling fingers over the valley between his shoulder blades.

He knows I know.

But we've also spent the last five years never mentioning it.

Until tonight. Because I suspect under the bow tie and the deep infatuation, I'm an idiot.

"I mean—"

He looks toward the movie screen. "I'm long over Roch."

I want to believe him.

But I'm slammed with the memory of Mort in the driver's seat, cap resting over his face, "Yesterday" blasting through the wagon. Then I'm slammed with more memories . . .

The movie starts and Mort turns up the audio.

We've seen the film before, but we've never seen it over dinner in the privacy of a car. My thoughts skip to best friends and unrequited crushes.

Hypothetically. *Can* two gay guys just be friends? Or will sex always interfere?

"What?" Mort hums.

I jerk my gaze back to the screen. "I love this bit."

"The wave at the New York Giants game?"

"It's poignant."

"The wave?"

"Yes."

"Yeah, okay. I'll bite. Why is it poignant?"

"Well, Harry is clearly depressed but he does the wave

anyway. It's like life. No matter how down in the dumps you are, you've got to keep rolling."

Mort turns down the audio. "Are you down in the dumps?"

I groan. "None of my conversations are going where I want them to go."

He speaks with sincerity. "If you don't feel like rolling the wave . . . I'm here to talk to."

I rub my milkshake-numbed thighs. "Thanks. Likewise. If you want to talk with me. But don't expect wisdom. Clearly don't. Listen to me. Crap—" My throat tickles, my lungs rattle, and I cough violently.

Mort squeezes through the gap between the seats and starts rubbing my spasming back. "Nice and easy."

His fingers scrape over my inner thighs as he plucks my milkshake. He takes off the lid and presses the rim to my mouth. I gulp the shake, relieving the worst of the cough and none of the embarrassment.

I sink back and slam my eyes shut. He stirs next to me, his elbow brushing my arm, his leg burning a pulse into mine.

I peek through my lashes and find him watching me. "What?" I hum.

"I do want your advice on something."

"At your own risk." I twirl a finger to signal the go-ahead.

"Tiffany."

"Tiffany, what?"

"That's what I want advice on. Tiffany. How do I get her on my side again?"

I groan. He's less in control than he'd like to know.

Show me you're truly happy with Mort around, and I'll be happy he is too.

"She needs time," I hedge. "She'll get there, you'll see." I point to Harry and Sally on screen. "We should watch the movie."

We continue to watch, side by side.

"You're not paying attention, are you?" Mort's voice in my ear tickles.

"Sure I am. They're about to have a miserable blind double date."

"Have you ever been on a blind date?"

Eyes rooted to the screen, I'm keenly aware of my clammy palms, nape, backs of my knees. "I haven't even been on a non-blind date since my first girlfriend."

Mort shifts, bewildered. "Not since *university?*"

I refuse to make eye contact and steal my milkshake back.

"But you're so . . . Damn. Are you shy? Uninterested? Unlucky?"

Let's go with that. "Yes."

He nudges my arm. "Shy and unlucky I can help you with, if you want."

What I want is to drown in this milkshake.

"We can go clubbing when you're feeling better. Next weekend."

I choke on a dry laugh. "You're hilarious."

"It'll be fun."

"We have different definitions of the word."

Mort lowers the volume. He wants to further this conversation. I nervously cough against a curled fist and Mort steadies my jerking milkshake. He frees it from me again. "Are you afraid to meet someone who makes your heart hitch?"

"Of course I'm not afraid to meet someone who makes my —heart hitch? Really?" I cock an amused brow at him and he holds my gaze, unnervingly steady.

"I'm not afraid of a few romantic words, Felix." He crinkles into a teasing grin. "At least, not as afraid as you are to step out and meet someone."

"I'm not afraid to meet someone, because meeting someone just won't happen. Not tonight. Not any night."

"Felix . . ."

"I've tried, okay? It's not shyness. I'm rarely attracted to women."

His quiet, unsurprised look sends all my nerves into a dive toward my feet. "And men?"

A hiccupping laugh tumbles from me, followed by a tingling flush. My voice is small, quiet. "Yes. Sort of."

"Sort of?"

"Well, I wouldn't be so quick to throw plurals about."

Mort absorbs this in agonizing silence. My eyes prickle as I resolutely stare at the screen.

A soft finger curves under my chin. I close my eyes and let Mort steer my face toward him. "Felix?"

I don't want to open my eyes, but I'm afraid keeping them shut admits more than I want to. Mort beholds me, his expression gentle and knowing.

Goosebumps rake over me.

Queries leap in his eyes, twisting and turning. My stomach ties his loose ends into knots. His finger slides under the unshaven base of my chin and my breath hitches, triggering a cough.

I rip my face away and cover my mouth. I have to stop this nerve-wrecking moment and make something abundantly clear.

I paste on a smile, shrugging. "I'm over you, Mort."

"Are you?"

I pause. "I will be."

He's quiet for a long moment, then he inclines his head. "Okay."

"Okay?"

"I wouldn't want anything more," he says stiffly. "I need to work on us. On mending our friendship."

"Friendship, yes. That's all I want. Not anything else. Ever. At all. In the world."

He eyes me, shuts his eyes, and hums. "All right, Felix. I

hear you."

"Good. Good. *Great.* Now turn up the audio."

Not three scenes later, Mort turns it down again. He spares me an inquisitive look. "Am I really the only man you're attracted to?"

"I thought you promised me greasy food, good view, and great conversation? This conversation doesn't feel great."

His laugh vibrates along the points we're pressed together; my bicep, upper thigh, the knob of my knee. "You triggered the scientist in me. I have curiosities. Questions."

I bang my head against the seat. "Maybe you're the only man. I don't know."

"We could . . ." He scrubs his jaw like he's trying to erase his slight beard. "We could check out singles night at Ivy. Flirt with some guys, see if there's any connection . . ."

I groan. "I don't need more proof that I can't find someone."

Mort looks puzzled. "More proof?"

I pick at invisible lint. "That guy we bumped into at Zealandia with your colleague Jack?"

"Ben McCormick?"

"He was the first and last guy I tried to hook up with. I thought maybe guys do it for me. What a disaster."

"What happened?"

"He was nice, and nothing." I steer my hot face toward the field of parked cars. "Not so much as a twitch."

Mort reflects quietly. "Maybe you're on the ace spectrum?"

"Considering the depraved fantasies I have while—probably not asexual."

Mort swears under his breath. Air puffs between us as he shifts an inch. "Maybe you need an emotional connection to someone first."

That sounds hopeful. Perhaps committing to dating someone would inspire attraction. "I don't know."

“As a scientist and someone wanting to be your friend again, I’m happy to hypothesize and test things out with you.”

He keeps emphasizing friendship and trying to draw a line between us. As if the Roch-shaped line wasn’t enough. Ha.

“At a gay bar?”

“Wherever you want.”

When the film is blessedly over, Mort chauffeurs me home.

My limbs shake as I climb out onto the pavement. Before I can take a step, Mort slides his arm around my waist and guides me to the front porch.

The house is dark—Mum and Tiffany likely in bed—but the porch light is blinding.

I sag against the wall of the porch nook, fingers digging into empty pockets. Mort, one step ahead of me, produces a spare key from underneath the fake rock in the lavender bushes.

Mort opens the door for me. He ushers me inside and follows me up the spiral staircase into my tissue-carpeted bedroom.

I slump onto my unmade bed and pry at my bow tie.

Mort motions toward me. “Are you good?”

“Getting undressed? Or with you watching?”

He stuffs his hands into his pockets. “Right. I’ll head.” He looks at me for a heart-quickening moment before twisting on his heels.

“Thank you for the outing,” I say. He pauses.

“Any time.”

He takes an inevitable step toward the door, and the evil butterflies in my gut try to rope him back. “Tiffany!”

Mort turns around, gaze seeking mine in the shadows of the room.

I tug my bow tie free. “She said she’d teach me to dance. For the wedding. If I found someone to dance with . . .”

His quiet, gravelly voice takes those evil butterflies hostage. "Are you asking me to dance with you, Felix Rochester?"

"Don't get the wrong idea."

"What wrong idea would that be?"

Playful dimples hop at the sides of his mouth. I never should have revealed my attraction.

I growl. "Yours are the only toes I have no qualms squashing."

He tips his cap and exits my room with an infuriatingly hot grin. "I look forward to it."

Chapter Twelve

FELIX

I FLY GROGGILY DOWNSTAIRS TO DROP THE GIRLS AT SCHOOL.

Mort is standing in the kitchen, sans cap, in a short-sleeved dark shirt and jeans stuffed into trekking boots. He's chatting to April and May across the kitchen island, smearing peanut butter over toast bread. Carrot peel and jars of marmite and jam litter the counter before him.

Luke-warm air shuffles into the house, but it does nothing to cool the heat searing my cheeks. Because of course last night rushes back to me in a groaning roar.

I want to sneak back into my room and pretend it was all a dream. I want Mort to claim he hit his head on his way to bed last night and remembers nothing of the past twenty-four hours.

Mort catches me gawking and delivers me an ultra-chuffed smile.

Clearly he's not forgotten.

If only he looked less good. If he didn't hold himself with that charming confidence that makes me want to press myself against him and absorb it into my soul. Maybe I could get over him faster and avoid the inevitable awkwardness.

My lungs rattle and I cough heartily.

"How are you feeling this morning?" Mort spins around and switches on the kettle.

"Like I want to die."

"And regarding your cold?"

I scowl; he laughs.

"How about you call in sick?"

"Are you cool"—I gesture to the lunches he's making —"doing all this?"

He slices ginger and drops it into a mug, fills it with hot water, and hands it to me. "I'm good with the kids. Your mum signed their museum-trip permission slips before she left for work. She wants you to rest up."

"She said as much?"

"I may be elaborating." His heavy laugh is quickly drowned out by April throwing herself at him.

"Please, please, please," she says, batting her eyelashes.

May pounces on me and starts begging too. "Please, what?" Mort and I say at the same time.

"Can we have a Halloween party next week?"

"A Halloween party?"

May nods. "To be super honest, this is mostly about the lollies. And checking out Jace and Coop's haunted house. But also, Mum loves it when we dress up."

"Isn't it enough that Christmas is around the corner?" I immediately regret my attitude. More than regret it. I need to give them attention. "I mean, Halloween. Hell, yeah."

Mort shakes his head at me.

"We're doing it?" April asks, glowing.

Mort inclines his head. "On one condition: you leave Felix to get better and let me organize it."

It takes until Saturday to completely kick my bug, and I've promised to work two weekend shifts to make up for the days off.

I peer out the living room windows. The Groove isn't parked out front like usual.

I turn, almost banging into Mum, who's dancing and humming cha-cha-chá. Tiffany is reading *Cosmopolitan* on the couch. We exchange wary smiles. Mum's in a good mood today too.

"Do you two want to cozy up on the couch and watch a movie?" Mum asks.

"I've got work." I hate to sound blunt, but I've sounded this way since Roch's engagement party.

If I could move past this aching vulnerability, I could talk to her about it. What if she doesn't accept me?

"Right. Well, have a good day, love. Tiffany?"

Tiffany sets her magazine on the coffee table and swings her legs off the couch. "Have you gone to the doctor to increase your dosage of fluoxetine like Felix keeps asking you to?"

Mum blushes under her thick make up. "Not yet."

Tiffany stands with an anguished press of her lips. "Then *not yet* to a movie."

My chest expands on a proud breath. Tiffany will be a strong, warm, fair-hearted woman. She *is* a strong, warm, fair-hearted woman.

Mum and I watch her leave the room. Mum turns her frown on me.

"I'll make you an appointment," I offer.

She swallows and nods. I want to fold her into a hug, but I can't bring myself to move.

~

Mort's childhood home is a downtrodden villa with a crumbling brick fence.

Mort calling my name startles me.

I turn toward the street. He climbs out of a charcoal Toyota and crosses toward me, firing a glance at his house that suggests he saw how I looked at it. He nervously resettles his cap.

"I figured you parked here." I motion toward The Groove across the road.

"Just finished the transfer of ownership. Dad's car will be picked up this afternoon."

"Oh, crap." I rock on my heels. "If this is a bad time, I can catch the bus."

He reaches out and braces my arm. "No, it's fine. I was about to drive up to you. Let me grab my wallet."

His broad frame kicks down the cracked path to his front door, tugging at my chest. I understand why Mort lights up when he sees our chaotic, colorful family.

Why he calls us his home.

My phone buzzes and I pull it out of my pocket.

A message from Mort.

Mort: It's just a house, sunshine.

I cross the street and lean against The Groove, typing back.

Me: How the hell do you read my thoughts like that?

Mort: You wear your heart on your sleeve.

Me: Yeah, well, you . . . dammit. I have nothing.

The front door snaps shut and Mort strides out the shitty gate, grinning at his phone.

Mort: When are those dance lessons happening?

I fire a text back.

Me: Been on your mind, has it?

Mort: Every. Bloody. Day.

I roll my eyes at him. "After Halloween. Now open the wagon."

He smirks, then slings himself inside. And I know I'm going to make his smile twice its smug size. I take a groaning breath, open the front door, and throw myself in the passenger seat.

I don't dare look at Mort, whose gaze washes over me.

"Don't say a word," I warn him.

"I wasn't going to. Not about how thrilled I am that you're finally in the front seat."

I whack his arm. "Only because I want more leg room."

He laughs, rich and deep. "Right. Definitely not because we're friends again."

I hitch a thumb toward the back seats. "You know how easy it is to climb back there."

"You forget."

"Forget what?"

He guns the gas and the momentum glues me against the seat. "I have physics on my side."

Chapter Thirteen

FELIX

HALLOWEEN.

Mort stands on our porch wearing a hooded black robe and gripping a pray-to-God fake scythe. A ginormous black duffel bag eats up the remaining porch space. Wind whips his hood. His long sleeves billow against my belt loops.

I open my mouth, and close it again.

His expression is all soft, I'm-at-home humor, and I brace my hands either side of the doorway, not to sink toward him.

I pin my gaze on his scythe.

His voice rumbles. "I'm the Grim Reaper."

"I see that. Why did you decide to dress as the reaper?"

"There are things I need to reap: a smile, a laugh"—He lifts his scythe and startles me into eye contact—"your undying affection."

I snort. "What did I ever see in you?"

Our gazes hold for a few beats until he ends the pulse-jerking torment. "Let me in?"

I take a rocky step away from the entrance, eying his attire again. "Mort. Death. Grim Reaper-ing. You love to take the piss out of your own name, don't you?"

"When shit dads give you shit names, you have to reclaim them for yourself."

The smile drains from my face, and Mort murmurs, "Ah, shit." He grips his scythe. "I'm okay, Felix. I never needed him."

He never needed his dad—who needed a dad who hated his son for surviving his wife? No, he never needed him.

He needed *us.*

Needs us.

I'm so fucking glad I reclaimed the front seat.

Mort follows me to the kitchen. I steady my breath and eye the bag on the kitchen island. "I'm all for partying, but the body bag makes me nervous."

He snickers, pulling out his phone from the jeans under his robe. "Roch and Lauren will be here any minute."

I jerk, banging my elbow against the island, and bleat a soft curse. Mort's fingers freeze on his phone, trying to make out what kind of clumsy move that was. Regular or flustered.

He slowly resumes texting. I rub my funny bone, trying not to focus on his phone.

Mort hums and I desperately want to know what he's reading.

Don't ask, don't ask, don't—"Have you been chatting with my brother a lot, then?"

I fiddle with the braided hem of his bag.

He tucks his phone away and speaks hesitantly. "He's still making me call him Michael. Our relationship is not what it was."

"But you hope it soon picks up where it left off?"

His expression stills. "I do."

So this night is really to *reap Roch.*

I nod. This bow tie is choking me. I loosen it and rip toward the hall, donning a smile. "Before everyone arrives, I have a mountain of laundry and . . . other chores. The twins are dressed in their room. I'll leave you to bond."

"Fat chance, Felix." He ensnares me with his scythe and draws me in. My belly takes a dive. I'm being totally obvious. Alongside this disappointment, I should feel embarrassed.

I should also quit acting so weird. "I don't have a costume," I blurt.

Mort presses the fake blade against the small of my back, nudging me forward. He nods toward the bag. "I raided the school theatre. I have costumes for you, Tiff, and your mum."

I scrounge around for another reason not to do this. "I don't have lollies!"

Mort reaches forward, hooking the bag with the scythe. My breath suspends at the sudden wall of warmth in front of me. He smells faintly of dry grass and lemons.

I rip my focus to the bag, watching the sides slacken as it opens.

Alongside heaped costumes are Cadbury chocolate bars and packets of licorice.

Mort lifts his brow at me.

God, he's so close.

Heat races to my cheeks. Races other places, too. "I don't . . . have any other excuse."

"Tonight you're going to have fun, Felix. Whether you like it or not." He leans in and whispers. "And I'm still waiting for a date."

"A date?"

"For our first dancing lesson?"

"Right. That." A panicked laugh shoots out of me, then fizzles.

Mum steps into the dining room, gleaning a direct view of our nose-to-nose encounter.

I'm sure I should flinch, but I remain paralyzed.

Mort calmly inclines his head. "Dolores."

"Mort."

They stare at each other, engaged in a silent conversation. Mort determined, Mum conflicted.

Mum settles an uneasy gaze on me.

I pretend to be interested in a *Where's Waldo* red-and-white striped fabric in Mort's bag.

Mum's voice has me tensing. "Felix . . . have you seen April and May?"

The girls burst into the kitchen. April's blue shirt says BASIC, May's red shirt says ACIDIC, and I don a never-been-so-glad-for-my-nerdy-jock-sisters-interrupting-me grin.

They engulf Mum and Mort in hugs. I make a dash for the bathroom.

When I dare return, Tiffany is raiding the body bag.

A spooky soundtrack echoes ghostly noises. The scent of popcorn wafts from the microwave.

Tiffany wedges on a cop hat, puffing her wavy hair. "What does this remind you of?"

I scowl. "I'm never getting pulled over again." She throws a black mesh tutu at my chest. "Ballet dancer?"

"A dancer who lost his Groove."

"I want you to have fun, Tiff. But you are having *too* much fun."

Her mouth quirks. "Tutu on, lead the way to this party."

All faux confidence, I stride into the living room, where May and April enthusiastically smear face paint and glitter over Mum's grimacing face while Roch and Mort light fake pumpkins at the windows.

Roch leaves Mort with the pumpkins and rounds the dining

table toward me. He's dressed in a safari shirt and red cap. He's dressed as Mort, and it's perfect.

He pulls me into a quick hug.

My tutu squashes against his waist and I hurriedly pull back to adjust it. "Where's Lauren?"

"She's not feeling well."

Sympathy shades Mort's eyes. "I hope she doesn't have what Felix had last week."

"You feeling better, Felix?" Roch feels my forehead, mothering me like a big brother.

"Fine," I bite out.

"I'm sorry I've been so busy. I can take the twins to soccer this weekend. After Christmas, I can see about doing regular pickups—"

"We have a routine!"

Roch frowns at me. Mort flashes me a more astute expression.

Heat lances up my neck. Crap. "I mean, yes, absolutely, thanks."

I lunge back into the quiet kitchen, only to have Roch follow me.

"Felix. I know I promised to take Mum to her doctor appointment tomorrow, but I cannot reschedule my meeting with the minister of justice at noon. Can we shift it by an hour?"

He's kidding, right? "Roch, we really need this to happen."

My brother snags a beer out of the fridge. "I calendared my meeting wrong. I was going to call earlier. I really can't, but—"

He grabs a second beer and slips into the living room again.

Well, shit. I know how he plans to resolve this.

I chase after him, but I'm too late. The question escapes Roch's mouth as I scooch into the room.

Mort accepts the beer and takes a sip. "I didn't know," he says, gaze shooting to me, questioning, gently disappointed. "Of course I'll drive her, Michael."

The foreign sound of Roch's given name stills Roch and I.

Roch frowns, twisting his red cap nervously. "Roch," he corrects quietly.

Mort's nostrils flare on a slam of emotion. My insides somersault out through my feet.

I pirouette to the twins and pray my voice doesn't stick. "Who wants to go trick or treating?"

Chapter Fourteen

MORT

HALLOWEEN IS NO BIG DEAL IN NEW ZEALAND. SOME YEARS, the Rochesters don't even stock up on candy. But our neighbors and friends Jace and Coop faithfully celebrate Halloween like it's a religion, decorating their glass mansion as a horror house.

Roch, Felix, and I take the girls to indulge in Halloween shenanigans.

Coop and Jace welcome us into the house with delighted, it's-been-too-long cries.

A couple years older than me, we didn't hang out much at school, but I roomed a year with Jace at Otago and we forged a solid friendship. Solid enough that he admitted he had complicated feelings about his step-brother. Solid enough that he cried admitting to dating his then boyfriend because he looked so much like Coop. Because he could imagine he *was* Coop . . .

"We're in Europe until your wedding, Roch," Coop says, sinking a hand into Jace's back pocket and tugging him toward the grand piano. "But after, should we all do weekly dinners again?"

Coop tells us to explore and Jace pounds out *This Is Halloween* on the ivory keys, not looking away from Coop the entire piece.

Felix races through the haunted house with the twins, his Chucks slapping over blood-smeared wood in his hurry to put distance between us.

I get it.

This is the first time Roch, Felix and I are hanging out together again. The dynamics have shifted—are shifting still.

Roch shoulder-bumps me. His dark, forgiving eyes wallop me with guilt.

My best friend has re-gifted me the use of his nickname and wants us to play DDR until dawn. Meanwhile, I'm fighting the urge to chase his brother and ask why Felix didn't ask *me* to take Dolores to her appointment.

A corpse bride bursts out of a closet and Roch startles. I bite down a smirk. Roch mutters, then shoves the hood of my costume over my head.

Laughter rocks out of me. Felix glances at us, revealing a flurry of emotions I don't need a science kit to dissect: jealousy, frustration, and gut-yanking sadness quickly masked with forced aloofness.

He's trying to get over you.

I don't want him to.

"Mort?"

"Hmm, yeah?"

"About the wedding." In my peripheral vision, Roch fingers the corpse bride's veil. "I was speaking with Lauren about it, and we want you—"

My attention rivets to Roch, and I throw up a hand. "Stop."

He freezes. "I thought you wanted an invite?"

"When I repair things with everyone in the family. I haven't done that yet."

"You've been trying. That's what matters."

I grind my scythe against the floor as I try to explain. "Look, I want to be at your wedding more than anything—"

"So consider this your invite."

"—but I need to feel like I deserve it. I fucked up. Big time, and I'm still working on us. On you and me. On me and the twins, Tiffany, your mum. And Felix."

"You want me to wait with the invite until . . .?"

I understand he needs to plan things. But I'm determined to at least win Tiffany over before I accept his invitation. "Can you ask again at Christmas?"

Roch chuckles. "That's what Felix said when I asked if he'd bring a plus-one."

I swallow the temptation to glance in Felix's direction. I can't swallow the possessiveness that simmers at the thought of Felix taking someone else. "And?" I choke.

"I'll ask again at Christmas."

Thoughts tangled in knots, I finish the rounds through the house and head outside. Felix has disappeared—I saw him leave ten minutes before the rest of us—and Roch is scaring April and May down the sidewalk.

I glimpse movement inside The Groove.

I motion for Roch to walk ahead. I rest my scythe on the letterbox and throw open the door.

Felix lets out a grunting yelp. "Are you trying to kill me?"

"Well, I'd be a bad reaper if I didn't try." I climb in.

I shut us into the dark car, absorbing the silence. Felix tilts his head against the headrest, gaze pinned on his mum's Honda parked in front of us.

It aches in here. Like being at home.

"Felix?"

"Yes?"

"We're putting on a movie inside."

"I'm good in here."

"It's lonely in here."

"Not lonely. Quiet."

"No, it's lonely."

"You can go back to Roch."

I scrub my jaw. Staying with Felix will launch a war inside me as I fight against my overwhelming attraction to him. But . . . I can't have him out here alone. I push aside my cloak and wedge my phone from my pocket.

"What are you doing?"

I don't answer. I send Roch a message to start the movie with the kids. Without us. "Pass me the car keys, mine are inside."

"What?" Felix gives me a startled look.

I brace one hand on the passenger seat and climb over the console. I slide my foot between Felix's legs. Felix's chest expands on a sharp inhale.

I shift my weight toward the driver's side, my shin locked against the seat.

I bore my gaze into his. "Give me the keys and move into the passenger seat."

"You could have gone around the car."

I'm barely refraining from kissing him. No way I could've gone around the car. "And have you lock me out? Not risking it."

He whimper-laughs. "What do you want?"

I reach under his tutu and palm his pocket, scraping his erection. He jolts under my touch with a strangled whine and I jerk my hand to the side. My cock hardens. I smooth over the tight fabric of his jeans, feeling the ridges of keys. "I want your keys, and I want to know why you didn't ask me to drive your mum."

"Stop looking at me so intently."

I can't. "I won't."

Felix slams his eyes shut. "Mum's always stiff with you, and what with her casting you out of our family—" Felix snaps his mouth shut. "I didn't think you'd want to drive her."

I tip his chin up and he looks at me guardedly. "Dolores finally told you the truth?"

He eyes the street like he's searching for an escape. "Maybe not *told* me, but . . . the words came out of her mouth and I heard them."

I've known Felix forever, and I know he's hedging the truth. "You overheard me at Roch's engagement party."

"Yes."

"You didn't say anything."

"No."

"It's almost November."

He folds his arms defensively. "It's almost November, and *you* still haven't told me."

"You know."

"You didn't know I know."

He's right. Awkwardly, I pull my other leg over the console and perch on his thighs, knees placed either side of him. The heat of his legs burns into my ass. His shiver vibrates through me. "Ah, Felix."

He arches his hips, diving a hand into his pocket. I inhale sharply as the movement rolls over my erection.

Felix obliviously presses the jingling metal against my chest. "When were you going to tell me you didn't know I was her donor?"

I clutch the keys. "I'm sorry. I didn't want it to seem like I was justifying my bad decision. I should have been here regardless." I straighten his bow tie, hoping I convey what I can't articulate.

He slithers out from under me, propelling himself onto the passenger's side. I'm left staring at the back of the seat.

I twist around slowly. Now I'm the one staring at Dolores' car to avoid Felix's gaze. "Will you talk to Dolores about it?"

"There's a lot to unpack."

His mum's deception, how she feels about me being gay, and if she truly hates it, what does that mean for him? "A lot, yeah."

"But I will. I need to."

We quietly study the Honda, the dashboard, and the gear-stick between us.

"Would you have stayed if you knew I was in hospital?" His voice sounds small.

Mine sounds smaller. "In a heartbeat."

He clears his throat. "Right, then."

"Yeah."

We glance at each other at the same time.

"Will you take Mum to her appointment, Mort?"

"You bet."

Felix grips the handbrake and releases it, and I drive.

DOLORES' DOCTOR APPOINTMENT HITS MY LUNCH BREAK.

I'm glad for the rain beating down on the roof and the swishing of wheels through puddles, because otherwise the silence would feel even more strained.

The car already feels strange without Felix peeking at me from the back.

I reach into the back seat and offer Dolores a paper bag. "Chicken sandwich and blueberry muffin."

"That was unnecessary." Her red polished nails gleam dully as she accepts the bag.

"I wasn't sure whether you'd have eaten lunch or not."

"Well, no. I haven't. Thank you."

We don't speak for the rest of the drive. We arrive ten minutes early and stare at the rain as she finishes eating.

I grip the wheel. "Why don't you take your Honda anymore, Dolores?" Why don't you help Felix take care of things?

"I'm afraid of having an accident. I'm . . . I'm afraid of everything." Her hoarse voice floods with sincerity, but it's still frustrating to hear.

"Mort . . ."

"Yeah?"

"When I was sick, when I thought I was dying . . ." She looks at me regretfully. "I bargained."

"Bargained?"

"If I lived life like He tells me to I should . . . I'd recover."

"And if you don't live like that?"

"I'll be taken away from everything I love."

I choke on a painful lump in my throat. "That's why you cast me away? To uphold your bargain?"

She stares at her lap. Long, tense moments pass—a silence so heavy and sad that it suffocates.

"Don't let fear drive away your family," I whisper.

She turns her carefully made-up face toward me, and I watch the rain.

"Believe me," I continue. "I lost them once, it's only painful."

She folds the paper bag, catching my eye. "Are you and Felix—"

I grind my palm against the wheel. "Don't go there, I beg you."

"I have a right to know if my son—"

"No. You don't have a right to anything. You have to work for your relationships like everyone else."

She blinks hard, eyes glistening. "I . . . yes. You're right."

I hate to see her hurting. Although *this* Dolores hasn't earned my love, the old Dolores is there somewhere, and I'll love her forever.

My throat tightens. I wish love weren't so difficult. "Take care of your mental health, let us help you. Reconnect."

"Today's a start, I hope."

I nod. "I hope. I'll be waiting here when you're done."

She zips her jacket and cracks open the door. The sound of rain intensifies.

I touch her elbow, and she pauses. "Every day I come into your house, I make the decision to forgive you." I smile sadly. "It's not an endless well."

She opens the door and dashes toward her doctor's office.

I dwell in frustration for a few minutes before distracting myself with grading. When I'm done ticking through them, I pull out my phone.

Me: You never gave me a date.

I expect Felix to be busy at work, but the three jumping dots say otherwise.

Felix: A date?

Me: For dancing. Are you on lunch break?

Felix: That's better than toilet break . . .Yes, I'm on lunch break.

Felix: How's it going with Mum?

Me: Sobering.

Felix: Thank you for driving her today. For driving us around last night.

Me: Any time.

I upload a new profile picture of myself. Within seconds Felix messages.

Felix: You bored, Mort?

Me: Take a photo and return the favor. I'm sick of your blank profile pic.

Felix: While I'm on the toilet?

Me: I don't give a shit where you are. ;-)

Felix: Good thing I'm getting over you, because any potential romance just slipped down the drain.

Laughter punches out of me and I recline in the driver's seat.

He doesn't upload a picture, but his next message makes up for that.

Felix: What about a dancing lesson next week?

Me: Too far away.

Felix: This weekend?

Me: Still too far away.

Felix: That only leaves tonight.

I grin at my phone.

Me: Now we're talking.

Chapter Fifteen

MORT

Felix lets out a relieved breath when "All of Me" by John Legend fades out.

He's wearing the same dark shirt and bright blue bow tie that he wore to work. One hand clutches mine, the other trembles against my shoulder blade.

The low sun casts purple shadows over the Rochesters' back yard. A wide glowing arc of outdoor light streams over the grass.

Tiffany sits on the porch streaming music through a speaker. "Got to grab my charger."

She disappears. Felix, to my bemusement, still doesn't let me go.

He tosses a lock of hair out of his eyes. "I wasn't totally uncoordinated."

"At our first waltz?"

He delivers me a dry look. "What else are we doing?"

"Good question."

He scowls at my grin. "The waltz, yes."

I pump his shoulder. He realizes we're still poised to dance and starts to pull away. I fasten our grip. Not yet. A little longer. "You were improving by the end of the song."

"When I started trampling your feet?"

"When you closed that boxy gap we started with."

A gentle flush tints his face and he bows his forehead against my shoulder, grinding it over my muscle. It feels good, him so close. It feels closer to dancing than what we've been trying to do. The ache I have for him couples a dull alarm for caution.

His voice skates down my open collar, eliciting a shiver. "I was totally bad at our first waltz."

I use my teacher voice in a strained effort to keep things platonic. "Ah, but you see? That's what practice is for."

"You're My Best Friend" by Queen leaps from the speaker. Tiffany emerges from the kitchen.

"Is this Roch's wedding playlist?" Felix squeaks. "Can't we just have instrumental music?"

"I like this song." I wink at him. I'm seriously struggling. "You're my sunshine."

"But not your best friend. Tiff, please."

My insides become immediately heavy. I don't know what to say.

We're not best friends.

But I have the inexplicable urge to call bullshit.

Inexplicable, because: he hasn't even outwardly admitted we're friends yet. Because, where does that put me with Roch?

A classical waltz begins to float out of the speaker. Felix steps a beat too early and stomps my toes. I take it with a wincing grin, but thank God I'm wearing boots. Maybe not the best to dance in, but a great shield against adorable, overeager monster feet.

Tiffany stops the music and kindly repositions Felix. She touches his upper back. "Keep straight and don't pull your shoulders up."

Felix gives a panicked snort, eyes flashing to mine, and I swallow a chuckle, squeezing his hand.

Tiffany nods her chin stiffly at me and shoots a pointed look at my feet. "I'm surprised you haven't cried yet."

She returns to her spot and the music restarts.

"I can't tell if that sounded impressed or regretful," I murmur to Felix.

He considers it, mischief sparking in his eye. "Bring on the tears, and we'll see if she grins."

I'm half tempted.

Felix counts under his breath as we step, tripping only once. "It's not only because of my two left feet, Mort."

"What's not?"

"Why I'm so bad. *One-two-three. One-two-three.*"

"Two left arms and no swivel?"

His hand shifts against my shoulder blade, warming the area an inch lower. "Yes. And we don't usually swap breaths like this. Well, last night too, but . . . you know what I mean."

"Are you saying carbon dioxide is throwing you off your dancing game?"

His flustered gaze hits mine with an electric spark. "I'm saying you make me dizzy."

Felix's eyes dart around the garden, Adam's apple bobbing, hand clammy against mine.

It's sobering, how he doesn't cloak his attraction in excuses and lies like I've been doing. Yet he holds back as much as I do.

"Just to be clear, why are you trying to get over me?" He misses a beat and I pull him into the right step. His head blocks the light streaming from the house, haloing his dark hair gold. From this angle, it's impossible to catch how blue his eyes are, but they are wide and fastened on mine. "Because of my history with Roch?"

Felix swallows. His voice is soft and serious. "Because even if you did like me back, I won't be your Rochester consolation prize. I would never know if, while you were with me, you were thinking of him."

That uncertainty would cripple anything more than friendship.

I lift my hand off his shoulder and scrub my jaw. Hard. I shouldn't feel disappointed. Shouldn't be thinking up ways I could prove otherwise.

This is a good thing.

Felix continues. "Mostly because I remember how much you drive me crazy."

"Quite the chauffeur I am."

The song ends, and Felix hurriedly lets go.

"Help me win Tiffany over?" I ask. His ruffled expression turns to relief.

He watches his sister unfold from the threshold. "There's not much *you* can do."

"I have to try."

"No, I mean—never mind. Convince her to practice driving."

"Done."

He snorts. "It won't be easy."

I'm not sure it will be either. "Don't forget my impressive greasing qualities."

Felix folds his arms and shakes his head at me, but his cheek twitches with a dimple. "If you can lure her into the driver's seat, I'll anoint you the Great Greasing Guru."

"Anoint, eh?"

"I'll bow down before you."

Jesus Christ.

Tiffany approaches and takes my hand. She leads me in a slow waltz, making Felix watch our feet.

It's the closest Tiffany has ventured to me since the prodigal *de facto* son returned. She steers me around, chin high, face schooled.

Over her shoulder, Felix watches me with a challenging lift of his eyebrow.

I smile at Tiffany. "I have a month off during the summer."

"That's nice for you."

"How would you like driving lessons?"

Her gaze whips to mine. "Felix? Why is Mort asking me this?"

"Because he doesn't know about your driving con list."

"I-I don't want to learn to drive," she says, frowning.

"Why not?" I ask, folding as she leads me into a panicked waltz. "What's on your con list?"

"Car accidents. Getting lost. Being pulled over." She throws Felix a pointed look, then continues. "The river flooding and being stuck in a car. A tsunami. Car accidents. Breaking down in the middle of nowhere. Breaking down in the middle of traffic. Driving at night. The seatbelt trapping me. Black ice. Spending all my savings. Oh, and did I mention car accidents?"

"Those things can happen whether you're in the driver's seat or not," I say.

Her eyes widen. Felix shakes his head, groaning.

"What I mean is: you'll be in more control if you're the one at the wheel."

Tiffany hesitates, fear lurking in her dark eyes, but there's also a spark of curiosity. Excitement.

"It's good that you're wary of the road," I say quietly.

She halts our waltz. "You don't think I'm ridiculous?"

"Recognizing your fears is the first step to dealing with

them. I can't promise those things won't happen, but I can teach you to drive safely. Defensively."

"I—" she snaps her mouth shut.

"We can take it slowly."

"How slowly?" she asks.

Felix eyes us, mouth slackened in surprise.

"Slow as you like."

Tiffany pushes us farther from her brother. "You seem to be fixing things with Felix."

"I'm trying to fix things with all of you."

"He's the heart of our home, Mort. He keeps us all running."

I've imagined a thousand different scenarios why giving in to my growing attraction to Felix was a bad idea. All of them come down to the words Tiffany next utters: "If you fuck anything up with him, I guarantee you'll lose every one of us."

I look her in the eye. "That's the last thing I want."

Her shoulders relax. "How about you encourage Felix to overcome his fear of dating—maybe help him land a plus-one—and I'll work on overcoming my fear of driving."

I swallow, nod.

She pushes Felix toward me. "I'll definitely think about those lessons. Felix, focus on your footwork."

Felix nearly slams into my chest, and his cooled fingers slide against mine. His eyes narrow, nose crinkling in disbelief. "What the hell kind of magic are you made of?"

"She's far from forgiving me."

"You persuaded her to consider sitting behind the wheel. Do you know how long I've been trying to do that?"

"Since she was sixteen and eligible to drive?"

"Well, yes, exactly."

Music plays and Felix hits the right beat, smoothly leading me into a waltz, fingers boring into my back.

"I guess I have to bow down before you."

I grip the muscle of his shoulder.

He pauses. "Or maybe later. Without an audience."

It's my turn to count steps, and I sound an awful lot like *Family, Felix, Fuck.*

When the music stops, I resist the urge to straighten his bow tie. "Tomorrow night."

"Tomorrow night?"

"Let's go to a gay bar. Find someone that makes your heart hitch. Someone you can imagine taking to Roch's wedding."

His breath skips over my chin, and his words punch into me. "I think I need that too."

Chapter Sixteen

FELIX

MORT IS RIGHT. I NEED TO PUT MYSELF OUT THERE. BUT THAT doesn't stop my trepidation.

I can barely stand still. I chase April and May's soccer game, hawk-eyes on the ball, but I hardly see it. Fighting the sweat on my neck, I imagine breaking out of my bubble.

Because that's what I will be doing tonight.

No more busying myself with chores and convincing myself I have my life together.

I'm stepping out of my safety zone and into an awkward mess.

Will I introduce myself to other guys tonight? Will I freak out like I did last time? Do I even *want* to hook up?

Will Mort be my wingman? Will he guide me through the night?

I really have to get over him.

A hand lands solidly on my shoulder and squeezes. I jerk

on my heel, lifting a clump of grass. Mort. Of course. Easy posture, legs spread slightly, and absurdly gold-hazel eyes like freshly cut wood sparkling in the afternoon light, lashes exceptionally thick. Afternoon stubble darker in the cleft of his chin.

"You okay there, Felix?" Mort tilts his cap and analyzes me.

I scrub my hands over my face. "Yes, of course. Why wouldn't I be?"

"Because the game is over and you're still pacing the sidelines?"

April and May are already walking toward the wagon, arms slung around each other's shoulders.

Right. "Just . . . warming up. For all that dancing tonight."

His expression shadows and he quickly schools it. "It's okay if you're nervous."

"Plenty guys in this situation wouldn't be. And I respect guys who can saunter into a bar like they own it. In fact, it's kind of hot. But, Mort, look at me." I hold up a shaky hand, failing to keep it steady. "I'm not one of those guys."

Mort grins, natural and easy. His charm is torture.

And in the same breath . . .

His torture is exquisite.

"This night is going to be a disaster," I mumble.

"Not with me by your side."

"How can you be so confident?"

Mort clasps my hand in his. "I'm one of those guys."

Mort drops April and May at Roch and Lauren's for an overnight stay. The idea came from Roch this morning, but I suspect Mort organized it behind the scenes. Probably in preparation for tomorrow, because two nine-year-old girls and a hangover don't mix.

Good thinking.

I'm absolutely not lying on my bed, staring at the golden sunset overflowing into my room, imagining Mort hanging out with my brother. Playing rounds of Dance Dance Revolution on his home console. Sweating, laughing, and play-punching each other. Roch properly whisking him into a slow waltz under the chandelier hanging from the vaulted ceiling. Eyes locking wantonly on Roch's unavailable ones. Mort drowning his painful longing in a beer as they make plans to hang out again soon . . .

I roll onto my side and check my phone. Seven, already.

What is taking him so long? I should have left the laundry to mold and gone with him.

I'm tempted to message him a reminder that I still exist. But. This is exactly why I need to go out tonight.

High time to get started on that.

I lug a dusty, half-empty bottle of whiskey to my bedroom along with an eggcup for a shot glass.

Pax Polo's *Best Of* collection blares from my speakers, creating a music ripple in my whiskey.

First shot. My throat is on fire.

Best to ditch the bow tie. Remove my shirt. Pants too. I'll need a more . . . fitting outfit for a night out. What, though?

Second shot. Whiskey spills onto my torso, tracking over the one-and-a-half-inch scar from last year's surgery. It's glossy, white, and smooth. I have mixed feelings about it.

But none of that tonight.

Third shot.

Thanks to a basket of folded—though not yet put away—clothes, I find the perfect outfit. I slink into the closet and study myself in the mirror. "At first you were afraid, you were—"

I fumble with my phone and soon I'm flinging my arms and mouthing the lyrics to "I Will Survive." Holy crap this song is everything. Everything.

Every scenario for tonight runs through my head: me

boldly approaching guys. Flirting with them. Asking them to dance.

I trip over my rug and fall onto the bed.

I grab the whiskey and uncap it.

I'm ready to throw my heart toward someone else. Ready to cultivate another crush.

Fourth, fifth, sixth shot—straight from the bottle.

Absolutely.

Chapter Seventeen

MORT

I SNATCH UP ROCH'S OFFER TO STAY FOR DINNER, EVEN THOUGH I have plans with Felix. A quick bite with my man here, and I'll be back at the Rochesters' in an hour.

With Lauren still cooped up with a box of tissues and classic rom-coms, we order in meat-lovers and apricot chicken pizzas and eat on the back deck.

April and May swing in a hammock tied between two Pohutakawa trees, eating their slices, while Roch and I shoot the usual shit: a rundown of soccer, cricket, and rugby. Roch's frustrations with his boss at work. My love of teaching at Kresley and the hope of extending my contract. A hike Roch wants to do up by Palmerston North. How The Groove is holding up and whether I'm tired of chauffeuring (not by a long shot), and fleetingly, if I'm interested in anyone.

I hesitate. "It's complicated." I wipe my greasy fingers and toss the napkin into the empty pizza box. "Thanks for the grub."

"You're not leaving already, are you?" Roch asks.

I'd been planning on it. I reach for the pizza box. "I'll have one more slice."

Roch takes the last one and chews the tip. "Complicated?"

"A dozen beers isn't enough to get into it—even vaguely."

"A dozen beers? We haven't had *any*."

"Exactly."

"Should I grab us some?"

"Not tonight, Roch." I pick the onions off my slice and take a cheesy mouthful. A large one. I can finish this piece in three bites. "Your brother and I are going out."

A bit of pizza falls from his mouth onto the deck. "For a second there, I thought you meant you and he were *going out.*"

I stiffen. I shouldn't ask, but curiosity gets the better of me. "That would be a problem?"

Roch doesn't hear it as a question. "Yeah, it would be weird. What with all the times we made out 'practicing'." Roch laughs, but it sounds forced. Maybe the memories make him uncomfortable. "Oh my God, you were never practicing, were you?"

Of course I hadn't just been practicing. Although now, I wish I had been. "You *practicing* on a guy gave me false hope for years."

Roch shifts and looks across the yard. "I thought we weren't conforming to that toxic straight dude bullshit." He bows his head, frowning. He opens his mouth and closes it again. Then clears his throat. "But, uh, I'm really sorry, Mort."

It doesn't bother me now. But there was a time when it did, and—

I understand why Felix is afraid of being the consolation prize.

I toss the rest of my pizza into the box. Fuck.

"Tiffany wants Felix to find a plus-one to your wedding," I choke out. "We're heading out to a bar for a couple drinks."

"So you're, like, my little brother's wingman?"

"Not so little, Roch. He's a man now. He has a job, he's managing the family."

"Christ. When did that happen?"

"When did he start doing all the household chores, providing love for all your siblings, and being a better person than the two of us combined?"

"When did he become a man?"

"The same time."

Pride glitters in Roch's eyes, but there's anguish there, too. "Fuck, I'll help out more. Somehow. It'll be easier after Christmas. Until then . . ."

"Until then, after then, I'm around to help."

He nods, and we eat the pizza in silence. April climbs the tree and hangs upside down from a branch, waving at us. We wave back.

"I forgive you," Roch says quietly. "For leaving. You've more than made up for it."

I crane my head toward the darkening sky and breathe in the sea-salted air. "Nothing can make up for my absence. But thanks for giving me a second chance."

We smile toward the back yard and absorb the sounds of the night: the call of an owl, the *yeow* of a cat in heat, the rustling of leaves, May pinching out a yelp from April.

When I finish my pizza, I push to my feet. "I have to head back."

I wish April and May a fun weekend and walk through the house. Roch snags my elbow as I'm about to hit the concrete path. His dark eyes shadow under the porch light and he rubs his nape. "I just. Ah. Next time you come around, spare time for us to haul out the PlayStation?"

I haul him into a quick hug. "You got it."

"And, um . . ."

"Yeah?"

"Make sure Felix has a good time tonight. He might be a man, but he's allowed to be a boy sometimes too."

~

I MUST BE SEEING THINGS. THERE IS NO WAY I AM FROZEN IN Felix's doorway watching Felix drink whiskey straight from the bottle, Tepid Creek's "I Will Get Over You" assailing my ears.

Except, I'm not seeing things. This is happening.

Felix dances, back to me, hips thrusting, head dramatically whipping in time. Whiskey jumps around in the bottle and I pray it was half-empty before he began.

He sings along, off beat and out of tune. He drops to his knees and sings: *so what you tasted of salted candy and a million dreams.*

God.

I focus on the tightly drawn blinds and peachy lamplight, his wrinkled but made bed, and the eggcup on the dresser next to his folded bow tie.

"Mort!"

Felix has swiveled in my direction and wears a stunned look.

I sink against the doorframe. "Guess you can cross off *bowing down before me* from your to-do list."

He scrambles to his feet, cheeks flushing. He tips the whiskey bottle toward his mouth but I pluck it from his sweaty grip.

He stares blatantly at me—*more* blatantly than usual—and I lift a semi-amused brow and measure how drunk he is. His eyes knock me with their blueness—not bloodshot, thank God. He's standing on his own, albeit with a slight sway. He smells of whiskey and caramel.

What exactly is he wearing?

Felix opens his arms and does a 360-degree turn. "What do you think?"

It looks like he squeezed into one of Tiffany's camisoles. The shiny black top sticks to his slim stomach, riding up half an inch on his hip. Half his V-line disappears under low-slung jeans. I almost drop the whiskey bottle. "What's wrong with your collar and bow tie?"

"I won't attract anyone at a gay bar wearing that."

"I beg to differ."

"What?" he says, and turns down his music.

I lean against his drawers and eye the camisole. "I said, it's not very you."

He flicks his bangs out of his eyes. "Isn't this whole evening about experimenting and hitching my heart elsewhere?"

I bite out, "Right."

He points at me. "Are you wearing that?"

"My usual jeans, shirt, and cap?"

"Your frown."

"I have a feeling you'll see more of it tonight." More than a fair bit.

"Better get used to it, then, huh?" Felix hums to whatever song is playing. He moves toward the whiskey but I shift a half foot to the right, blocking it.

He's thrown off balance, and I clutch his forearms, staying him. A dreamy sigh slips out of him and his mouth quirks. "You have nice, strong hands"—he shakes his head suddenly —"that you'll wrap around someone else's waist tonight. Crap. One last shot of whiskey?"

Ah, Felix. If you only knew.

If only we weren't so *afraid.*

I don't let him have the whiskey. My gaze fastens onto his nice, full, pouty lips—*that he might press against someone else's tonight.* "How about we stay in? Curl up on the couch? Watch a movie?"

"No. You have to take me to a gay bar. Help me get over you."

My frown is the Cotahuasi Canyon right now. "How about another time?" Or never. "When you haven't drunk anything."

"Please take me out tonight. While I have the courage."

Despite his pleading blue eyes, I gently peel my hands off him. "Ah, sunshine. Liquid courage isn't courage."

"It numbs the fear. Good enough for me."

I repeat Tiffany's warning in my head. "Sober up," I bite out, "and we'll go."

"Promise?"

Fuck, fuck, fuck. "Sure."

I clomp downstairs, slap together a few cheese sandwiches, and fill a bottle with water. When I return to Felix's room, he's checking himself out in the closet mirror.

He looks at my reflection. "Maybe this isn't 100% me, but I've watched TV. I know what hot guys wear to bars."

I gesture toward the food I brought. "Look. You'll look great, no matter what you wear. Do you feel comfortable? Are you okay with the fact your nipples are showing?"

He whips around and extends his arm. "Give me a shirt."

I laugh. "Come eat something."

"And a vest."

"Drink all the water."

He grabs a navy shirt and slips it on over the camisole, leaving the buttons undone. After washing a sandwich down with water, he lies on the bed, legs slightly spread, fingers working his buttons. His hair is strewn, cheeks flushed, thighs straining his jeans.

A soft yawn ripples through his body as he stretches.

Tiffany's warning is ringing weaker and weaker. I don't

want to take him to a bar. Don't want him mauled by anyone else.

Fuck.

Close your eyes, Felix. Fall asleep until tomorrow.

He doesn't though. One lip-synced Pax Polo album later, he's clumsily knotting his bow tie.

"Crap." Felix says abruptly.

"What's up, Felix?"

"You've done this before. Gay bars."

I hesitate at the trepidation in his voice. "Plenty of times."

He groans.

I lift a brow. *What?*

He hauls himself to his feet. "You're, like, *experienced.* And I'm all, like, Elmo Goes to a Gay Bar."

"You know what? Maybe Elmo Goes to Bed instead?"

He punches my bicep. I straighten my cap, hiding my hopeful smile.

"Maybe later," Felix says. "Now take me out for the night."

Chapter Eighteen

FELIX

"SHALL WE?" MORT ASKS.

"Absolutely," I answer, loosening the bow tie I donned before leaving the house.

We're standing on Cuba Street outside a sixties-looking former department store. No one seems to mind the chilly breeze.

Mort watches me patiently. I made him leave his cap at home, and beams of light brighten his short hair.

"You sure you're ready?"

I tug at my shirt and jerk a thumb at my chest. "Let's hitch this bitch."

"All right then."

I walk six steps and turn back at the door. Mort is still standing there, grinning crookedly. Like he predicted—hoped? —I wouldn't make it far.

I stomp back, pulling more at my collar. "You shouldn't

have sobered me up. I can't go in there. Great, my bow tie is lopsided."

I fiddle with the silk fabric, but my fingers are twitchy. I'm making a mess of it.

Mort swats my hands away and takes over. His breath trickles over my eyebrow. I focus on the glossy button at the open neck of his shirt.

I sway again. Hopefully it's from the whiskey.

"If you go inside," Mort says quietly, "I guarantee at least one guy will look at you and think you're incredible."

Reassuring. And nerve-wracking. A trio of neon-dressed guys emerges, one of whom unmistakably casts his eye over us.

In an instant, I'm sweating. Everywhere.

I swallow. "What if I can't return the sentiment?"

A chuckle puffs over my nose and Mort tugs my bow tie. "You mean look at him like you're . . . a little bit in awe?"

"Yes, that. Exactly that."

Mort lets go, gaze sweeping to mine. "Just be yourself and it won't be a problem."

"I hate the idea of leading a guy on."

Mort frowns. "Hey, you can flirt and have fun without the expectation of more."

"Yes, but—"

"No buts."

"Okay." I haul in a courageous breath. "Okay, okay." My feet remain glued. I grimace at Mort's athletic build. "Can you, I don't know. Carry me in there?"

He laughs. "Bridal style or flipped over my shoulder?"

"Piggyback."

"Works, too."

Mort grips my wrist, pulling until my armpit lodges over his shoulder and my chest presses against his back. He fishes for my other arm, his ass butting against my crotch. Both my arms looped around his neck, I finally find my voice. "What are you doing?"

"What do you think?"

"I was *joking*."

"I wasn't." He grips my wrists in one hand and claps my ass with his other, hefting me onto his back. My legs lock around his hips. He drags his hands down the back of my thighs and settles them under my knees. "Let's go."

Mort bounces me into the exposed-wood bar that features a ceiling of stringed, golden lights. Heads turn. I rut out a laugh, clutching his shoulders. His hair combs my lips. "We're making quite the entrance."

"We'll be memorable, then."

"Guys might think we're . . ."

Mort lets go of my knees and I slide off him. A flicker of *something* crosses his face. "We're what?"

My spine tingles. "Really drunk."

Mort quietly steps backward toward the crammed bar. "Okay, Felix. I'm here for you, but I want to be clear: you're making the rules."

I chuckle, unable to shake this sudden awkwardness. "Buy me a cocktail? Virgin." My nervousness makes the request sound more like: *Buy me a cocktail, virgin!*

More than a few pairs of eyes fly toward us and I walk backward toward the entrance.

Mort grabs my arm, laughing, and steers me across the room to buy us drinks.

The warm bar smells of sweet alcohol and sweat.

We're sitting at a high table near one end of the bar. From the other end a guy— glasses, jeans, and ripped Pride T-shirt —keeps checking Mort out. And behind him, another one—Maori, lean, half-shaven head—is checking *me* out?

Mort's knee nudges mine under the table. "You're not still upset about calling me a virgin, are you?"

Tiny bit, yes. "I probably did you a favor. Doesn't everyone want to jump the virgin?"

"Please. First-time sex is awkward and painful, it's way better if I know my partner is enjoying it."

"Does that mean you're a—I mean, you're experienced?"

Mort sips his beer.

"Sorry, that's too personal."

"No, I . . . yes. I'm experienced." His gaze flickers to mine and stays. "I prefer to top."

I swallow. "I feel weird."

"Weird how?" he asks, not looking away.

I try to shrug off the rising flush. "Kind of, um, vulnerable."

Softly, "Why?"

"This conversation."

"What about it?"

Everything. It's making me compulsively shiver and my dick hard.

I duck my head closer to him and hiss under my breath. "I'm a virgin, Mort." Mort finally averts his gaze and takes a long drink of beer. "You're telling me even if I *wanted* to hookup, no one will want to do awkward and painful with me."

He sets his glass down and twists it, leaving stripes through condensation. "When you have sex for the first time, I hope it's not a hookup." He looks at me again. "I hope the guy wants to do awkward and painful with you, because it will be the first of many times together. I hope you like it."

Shivers riddle me, shooting from the base of my spine to my throat. Under my shirt, I'm a canvas of goosebumps.

I jerkily reach for my cocktail and knock it askew. I overcorrect, and blue liquid lurches out of the glass, arcing toward Mort.

He shoves back from the table but not fast enough. My cocktail juice lands in his lap.

"Shit." I grab my napkin and palm his crotch, soaking up liquid. It's not enough. I dump the soggy napkin and grab Mort's.

Mort scrapes his palm over the slight bulge in his pants, pushing the liquid into the crack between his legs. "You're making it worse—wait."

I rub the second napkin over the seam of his pants, and Mort groans, clamping his thighs together. "It's fine. I've got it."

I wedge my fingers free from the warm prison and sink back against my stool, heat scalding my cheeks. "Could I be any clumsier?"

"Sure. You could have also tipped over my beer."

"Well give me a minute."

He accepts a donation of napkins from Glasses Guy who's been eyeing him. When he looks over at me, he must see humiliation burning my ears. "Don't worry about it."

"It's not just your crotch I'm worried about."

Mort's brow gives a funny twitch. "Oh, really?"

I glare at my emptied glass. "You could get lucky tonight. Instead you're keeping my nervous ass company. And your crotch is blue."

"It was already blue."

"Not pissed-your-pants blue."

"Felix, look at me." Reluctantly, I look. Mort wears a half-cocked grin and his eyes hit mine with another wave of shivers. "I'm feeling pretty damn lucky."

I rub my nape. It feels good hearing that. Too good. The kind of good that will land me in trouble.

The sexy scream of "Wild Thing" plays. Guys energetically drag their boy/friends to the dance floor, and I laugh at myself for letting butterflies get the best of me.

This song was on Roch and Mort's Air Guitar Classics playlist. Every morning, they'd scramble out of their shared bed and danced half-naked to Beastie Boys, Hendrix, and AC/DC.

I can still see eighteen-year-old Mort on Roch's bed riffing on the air guitar, thrusting his hips toward my brother at the bedside until Roch sweeps his knees and drops him on his back.

I can see Mort turning his head, laughter fading as he catches fifteen-year-old me staring through a crack in their door.

Mort seems to recognize the song too, because he shuts his eyes and breathes it in.

"I should put myself out there," I say over the swell of music.

He utters a curse. Did Roch's rejection hurt him as much as watching him pine for Roch is hurting me?

Mort's eyes open, dark and sad. His half smile is a grimace now. "Your rules, Felix."

My nod feels heavy. "I'm pretty sure the guy with the half-shaven head wants me."

"He's not the only one."

Half-shaven-guy kicks off the wall and weaves toward the exit. I reach for a gulp of Mort's beer.

The glass wobbles but Mort steadies it.

I bellow out a frustrated laugh. "See, I told you to wait." I give up on the beer. "Wish me luck."

If Mort does, I don't hear him over the roaring pulse in my ears and the *slitch* of my shoes.

Heat soaks between my shoulder blades where I feel Mort watching me. My step stutters. I curl fists at my side and force myself not to look back.

Half-shaven Guy gets waylaid by an incoming group and I catch him at the exit. He smirks, gesturing to the door. "After you."

"How about after a drink with you?" I blurt.

He arches a wicked brow. "Yeah, maybe."

"I'm Felix."

"Tane."

He's eyeing me up, and he's hot—flawless brown skin, high cheekbones, and broad shoulders that taper to a trim waist—but I'm not feeling anything, save wooziness from being near Mort all evening.

Tane jerks his chin over my shoulder. "Who's the guy you came with? You guys together?"

"Neighbors. Sometimes idiots. Currently, he's my chauffeur."

"And your bodyguard? Cause he's givin' me some pissed-off, don't-cross-me looks."

"That's just his face."

Tane keeps looking over my shoulder. "Uh, I'm not thirsty after all."

I glower at Mort. His jaw is a slab of concrete, and his expression is dark like he's shrouded in thunderclouds and unkind thoughts.

His eyes shift to me, and he visibly relaxes. He throws me a halfway smile.

I turn back to Tane to assure him not to worry—

He's gone.

I fold my arms and frown, trying not to feel so damn relieved.

It's clearer than ever that the million stars shooting around my chest need to be aimed at someone else.

I thread my way back to the table. "Well done, Mort, you scared him off."

"I did?"

"You did."

Mort offers me a sip of beer. I shake my head, and he drains the glass. "You want a repeat?"

I laugh drily. "Of which part? Calling you a virgin? Spilling my cocktail all over you? You scaring away guys interested in me?"

"Any of it."

I sigh. "Let's go home."

With brisk steps, Mort leads the way. Wellington Harbor glitters, and a crescent moon holds my attention whenever Mort catches me staring at his sugar-scented crotch.

I'm looking at the moon—a lot.

Argh.

I scrub my face and whimper-groan.

"What's up, Felix?"

Well.

Mort clears his throat. "What are you thinking about?"

I laugh darkly. "The bar scene isn't working for me. I'll have to try another approach."

I'll have to try a lot harder.

Chapter Nineteen

FELIX

THE NEXT MORNING, HANGOVER POUNDING IN MY HEAD, I agree to cover a co-worker's shift.

I shower, knock back some painkillers, and check online for the best Sunday bus route.

A shadow falls over my phone and I startle. "Mort! You stealthy bastard."

"I called your name, you hungover prick."

I laugh, immediately regretting it when pain ricochets around my head.

Mort lifts a brown bag. "I brought breakfast. What are you doing?"

"Planning how to get to work."

"Ouch, you got called in?"

"It's going to be fun day."

Mort insists on driving me. A golden sun hovers over the hills, the sprawled city glistens before us. Twice, Mort yawns and stretches, palms pressed flat on the roof. He looks wrecked himself. He hasn't shaved and his cap is hiding scrunched hair. He only had one beer, though, so his hangover must be from lack of sleep.

I didn't sleep much, either. Spent all night figuring out how to crush this crush. I have an idea that I might be able to start today . . .

I fiddle with my belt, plucking it like an instrument.

Mort shifts gears the moment the traffic light turns green. "Why are you squirming like you've ants in your pants?"

"I'm hungover and nervous."

"I know what made you hungover. What's making you nervous?"

"There's this guy at work."

Mort's gaze pins the road. "Are you talking about Jason?"

"I—yes, wait, how did you know his name?"

"You mentioned him a while back."

I try to recall. "The only time I remember mentioning him was the day after Roch's engagement party, when I didn't want you chauffeuring me."

"As I said, you mentioned him."

"You have a good memory."

Mort flicks the blinker and changes lanes. "For some things."

I chew my bottom lip, but a chuckle seeps out. "So, Jason. I was thinking since I know him, we might *connect* better."

Mort growls and honks at the car crawling ahead of us. "This is a fifty zone, and he's going twelve. I need music."

He turns on the radio.

I lower the volume. "Okay, you're tired and grumpy this morning, want to talk about it?"

He blows out a breath. "Sorry. You and Jason. Is Jason gay? Bi?"

"I think so."

"And you think he likes you?"

This is part of my problem. "How do you tell if a guy likes you?"

Mort rubs his hands up and down the wheel. "I usually find body language screams most answers. Like being followed by your best friend's little brother your whole lives . . ."

"Yes, but how can you tell they like you if they aren't crazy stalkers?"

Mort chuckles and side-eyes me. "Extended eye contact. It's a look. You learn to recognize it."

"Show me."

"I am."

"I can't tell. You look at me like that all the time."

"This is true." He returns his focus to the road. "Another way you can tell?"

"Yes?"

"If you flirt or mention someone else, they frown and withdraw. Maybe get pissed. And if you ask them to do something unreasonable, something they don't want to, they'll do it anyway."

Right. "Jason's there this afternoon. If you come inside to pick me up, I'll introduce you, and maybe you can observe?"

Mort glides into a parking spot outside the retirement home. "Yeah, I just don't want to."

"Too awkward?"

"That's one word for it."

"Fair enough."

His eyes hit mine, darkly frustrated and amused. "You're still hoping I do it anyway, aren't you?"

"If you take greasing seriously, this would be greasing me pretty hard."

"Damn it."

I grin, grab my shoulder bag, and leave the wagon. "Three-thirty, main entrance."

~

At three-thirty on the dot, after a pleasant yet tiring day taking care of residents, I see Mort strolling through the entryway. He removes his cap, stuffs it in his back pocket, and nods at my colleague. I hustle to greet him.

He's wearing slick pants, a dark shirt, and shiny shoes. Different outfit than this morning. "Crap, you look . . . incredible. Not exactly helping, Mort."

He laughs. I force my gaze not to stray over his length a second time. "Look, Jason is still in the lounge with his grandfather."

"Are we postponing the fun?" Mort asks brightly.

I roll my eyes. "By five minutes. We'll catch him on his way out. In the meantime . . ."

Mort glances around the warm-colored walls. "Show me the toilet?"

"The one I texted you from?"

"Any one will do."

"Oh. You need to *use* it."

He gives me a curious look. "What did you think I would do with it?"

"Wrangle me against the porcelain-tiled wall and shoot? With your camera. For my profile picture?" I thump his shoulder and steer him toward the bathroom, cursing. "Kill me now, Mort. Ha!"

Seriously. Kill me.

When Mort exits the restroom, I lead him toward the lounge, eyeing him.

"Why are you dressed up?

"Tiffany wants us to practice dancing. She thought these shoes would be better than the steel caps I suggested. You like?"

"More than Tiffany likes the idea of you having toes, obviously."

We bump into Jason leaving the lounge. He stops when he sees me, and a smile lights up his face.

I nod my chin casually, fingers sinking into my pockets. "What's up, Jasey?"

I have never called the man Jasey in my life.

Mort's eyebrows shoot to his hairline. Jason looks puzzled. "Just visited granddad. Like usual?"

"Yes, yes. I mean, how is that old man?"

Can I suck at this anymore?

"We played chess today. He loves it."

I lean back against the cool hallway wall. "And you, what do you love?"

Mort coughs violently behind a fist. Tears sparkle in his eyes, uncovering a giant dimple.

Jase's gaze latches onto Mort, and his posture straightens. And there. *There* is the look Mort was talking about. Delivered Mort's way.

Jason is definitely gay/bi then. And I am definitely not his type.

"Who's this?" Jason asks breathlessly, sparking an urge to jump between them and slap Mort against his chest so firmly he rocks back on his heels.

"He's my friend."

Mort makes a strangled-sounding grunt. His gaze burns through my profile.

Jason introduces himself, and—

"Wow. Time flies. We have to take Tiff to dance practice."

That is, if she had practice today.

I grab a handful of Mort's bicep and tow him down the hall.

Mort chuckles behind my ear and then calls back toward Jason, "*Really* nice meeting you."

We're barely strapped into The Groove when I shout, "Go! Go! Go!" As if we're hightailing from a crime scene, which I'm fairly sure the awkwardness we just left was.

Mort takes a new route. Fifteen minutes roasting in my embarrassed flush later, we're parked up Mount Victoria enjoying an incredible view of the sun-soaked city and sea.

Mort levels his twinkling gaze on me. "Where to start?"

I grind my head against the headrest and groan.

Mort unbuckles and swivels. "Actually, I'm starting with my favorite bit."

"Every bit was embarrassing. Every line as bad as the next."

"Except one." His cocky gaze reflects a thousand laughs. "'He's my friend?'"

I narrow my eyes, but my lips are hitching. "An annoying, gloating friend."

"You meant it then."

"I meant it *then*. Now, however . . ."

Mort catches my flailing hand and gently pulls my fingers until they're half-knotted with his, resting on the gearshift. "You're calling me your friend again."

It's suddenly hard to breathe. "This is redundant. Sitting in the front seat said that. Besides, you know about my stupid crush on you."

"Counts more when you say it. Less room for misunderstanding. And it's not a stupid crush."

No. I'm bloody well in love with him.

"Say it again."

I put on an exasperated sigh. "We're friends."

Mort grins, shifting back, fingers drawing away. "Where are the witnesses when you need them?"

I eye the phone he's suddenly holding. "I swear, if you call Roch, I'm denying everything."

Mort stabs his screen and holds the phone to his ear. His

grin widens. "Hey, Mort here. Yeah, good. I was wondering if you'd do me a solid? . . . I have Felix next to me and he's just told me we're officially friends again. I want to celebrate this defining moment in my life, and since you happen to be his 'absolute favorite rock star of all time,' I—"

I shriek, moving so wildly my seatbelt locks. "You called Pax freaking Polo?"

Mort fiddles with his phone, grinning. "You're on speaker, Pax."

"Holy crap," I say on repeat. A deep, cheeky laugh bursts from the speakers.

"Felix. What's it like having Mort back in Wellington?"

Like having your life turned upside down and relocated someplace with sketchy gravity. "It's fine."

"Fine?" Pax teases.

"Sometimes mediocre."

Mort slaps my thigh, shaking his head and silently laughing. His fingers rest on the inner seam of my jeans, palm blazing. It takes Herculean effort to focus on the rock star talking on the other end of the line.

"It's been four months since he left us in Dunedin," Pax says, "and he's barely called us."

"Well. He's not great at keeping in touch." Mort's palm slides away but I slap my hand atop his, pinning him to the seat. "But he knows how to make up for it."

"Thanks for the reassurance." Pax laughs. "We miss him but probably not as much as he missed you. He was always a miserable grump. He was always saying Felix this, Felix that."

"Oh, ah, I think you mean Roch." I laugh, freeing Mort's hand. I thread my fingers through my hair.

"Yeah, he moped about Roch too. And Tiffany, and the twins—what are their names again?"

"April and May. Don't ask who the older one is."

Pax scoffs. "People aren't that stupid, are they?"

"A teacher once asked when their birthdays were. So . . ."

"Our poor kids. Mort, could we pay you ridiculous amounts of money to come back and teach my daughter?"

"While your daughter is wonderful, I'll never leave the Rochesters again."

"A good friend, you have there, Felix," Pax says.

My dry tongue clucks.

"Now for the most important question," Pax says with an edge of mischief. "Did you crush on me growing up?"

Mort interjects. "We're about to hit some bad reception."

I lean forward. "I didn't crush on you growing up. But now that I've talked to you . . ." Mort oscillates between a laugh and a scowl. "Any chance we could fly to Dunedin and meet Pax in person? Maybe for my Christmas present?"

"Oh, would you look at that." Mort ends the call to Pax's charged laughter. "Can't hear you anymore."

I roll my eyes. "Thanks for calling Pax freaking Polo as a witness to our rekindled friendship. That's worth the rekindling on its own."

He hitches a brow. "Will you really crush on him?"

"If only it were so easy." I sink back as my humiliating afternoon plays back on repeat. "At this rate, requited love will never happen."

I admire Mort's pink lips and then the twinkling harbor.

Mort remains quiet a long beat, then speaks softly. "It'll happen, Felix."

"What makes you so certain?"

He restarts the car, and glances at me solemnly. "Just a . . . feeling."

Chapter Twenty

FELIX

DURING THE FOLLOWING WEEK, NEITHER MORT NOR I mention the weekend. Specifically, neither of us mention my failures at putting myself out there. With a shortage of staff at work, I take the bus into town to work extra shifts. Mort ensures that April and May arrive to and from school, and Tiffany to her dance classes. He also helps the twins with homework and drives Mum to the supermarket.

Three nights he makes dinner, ignoring my tired pleas to let me help—my ass meets the playful end of a wooden spoon whenever I try. *Just relax,* Mort says. *I'm a scientist.*

All I can do is lean against the counter, watching Mort as he produces thick-framed reading glasses and tediously follows recipes.

Friday evening, I stop by Tiffany's dance class.

Mort—all muscle and height—glides into the large studio

and sits next to me like a protective shield. Rugged to my coiffured. Handsome to my plain. Attentive to my distracted.

Tiffany and Arjun gracefully whisk about the room in a Viennese Waltz.

Mort leans toward me, sleeve brushing mine, voice low. "*That's* how it's supposed to be done."

I elbow him. His chuckle puffs at my temple. "Why are you watching with me, anyway?"

"Tiffany is really good."

"Yes, good swing and sway. Impeccable footwork." Mort blinks. "What? I may not know how to dance but I know how it looks . . . Shouldn't you be on Dance Dance Revolution next door?"

He focuses on the dancers. "I'm good."

Lauren frowns at us over the rise and fall of Tiffany and Arjun's steps. Mort and I quietly observe the class of passionate, athletic dancers. All six respect Lauren when she gives them advice, and they persist until they improve.

Mort fishes out his phone. Seconds later, mine vibrates against my thigh. I hop, glancing at Mort. He directs his attention to the dancers, but his grin is a little too playful.

I pull out my phone.

Mort: We should take a cue from these guys.

Me: Persist and perfect?

Mort: Each pair has weaknesses and fears. They acknowledge them, work on them.

Me: That's what makes them grow. Makes them amazing.

Mort: Exactly.

Mort stares at me as I read his message. The urge to swallow builds until I can't suppress it.

My phone buzzes again.

Mort: Help me sneak Tiffany into the arcade after?

Me: What for?

Mort: Our first driving lesson.

Lauren dismisses her dancers. I curl my face toward Mort. "In an arcade?"

Mort mirrors me, dipping his head. "Yes. Why are we whispering?"

"I don't know. I can't stop without feeling awkwardly loud."

"Okay, keep whispering, but I'm going to use my voice."

"Starting when?"

Shivers race through me at Mort's loud laugh. "Now, sunshine. Let's grab Tiffany and clear out."

Tiffany eyes us suspiciously as we purchase tokens. I eye Mort suspiciously as well. How is this meant to be Tiffany's first driving lesson?

We stop before Cruis'n World, a car-racing game featuring tracks around the world. Mort gestures Tiffany toward one of the two seats. "Lesson One."

She laughs incredulously and fingers the neck of the seat. "Racing?" She inclines her head toward me. "Is this how you taught Felix? That would explain a lot."

I tug her ponytail, and she pinches my arm.

Mort settles into one of the seats and Tiffany hesitantly lowers herself into the other. "Racing?" she asks again, quieter.

Mort studies her. "Confidence building."

"How so?"

"I'll talk you through every obstacle and close curve."

"Really?"

"By the end of the evening, you'll manage this without a single fender-bender." His smile makes my throat tighten with tenderness and frustration.

I murmur for them to have fun. I back down the aisle, where it's easier to breathe. Where I still have a good view of them.

Dance Dance Revolution blinks at me. I promise myself not to search for Mort and Roch's top scores. I slip a token into the machine and dance to *Always on My Mind.* I have no rhythm and miss most of the steps. I don't fare any better the second time around.

After the third, I lean back against the bolted bars to catch my breath. My phone vibrates and for a pulse-skipping second I hope it's Mort.

But it can't be, he's racing—and laughing—with Tiffany.

It's my brother.

Roch: What are you up to, little bro?

If I didn't love him so hard, I'd hate him for that "little bro" comment.

Me: Just whipped your old DDR score.

The lie flies out of my fingers.

Roch: Are you serious???

Guilt surfaces but I push it down. Roch will take my word for it. He's awesome like that.

Me: Hey, I've got some moves.

Roch: Never would have believed it. ;-)

Me: Ha. Ha. What can I help you with?

Roch: That's my question. Work is breezier next week. I thought I'd pick up the girls a few times—maybe pop around with Lauren and make dinner with you on Sunday?

Me: Super. Great.

What's not great, however, is scrolling through the top scores until MORT and ROCH wink at me from their first and second place perch.

I'm a glutton for emotional punishment.

A hand lands on my nape and I lurch around wildly.

Mort and Tiffany chuckle.

"We're done for today. Are you ready? Or would you like to dance a round?" Mort levels his gaze onto my screen and his expression shifts. He studies me. It's a brief moment, yet his eyes flicker and my chest constricts.

Stupid scores. I never should have looked!

I stutter. "N-no."

"They're just numbers," he says quietly, and I hate how shrewd he is. I hate that he knows it's the numbers 1 and 2 that knot me up the most.

I aim for a steady smile and shrug. I hook my arm around Tiffany's. "So, Tiff. What should we buy your sisters for Christmas?"

Chapter Twenty-One

MORT

I PARK THE GROOVE OUTSIDE THE ROCHESTER HOUSE.

It's just me and Felix. He stares at his knees, hair nearly covering one eye.

I've spent many sleepless nights in my empty house thinking about Felix and me.

I can't squash his show of possessiveness toward me in front of Jason. Can't stop remembering the heat of his thigh under my palm, the urgent snap of his fingers locking to mine during the call to Pax Polo. Can't erase the memory of Felix's glistening, frustrated gaze after being caught reading the DDR score screen.

Can't suppress the vein-tingling need to ease his mind.

The last few weeks of the school term have raced by as the decision has settled more firmly within me.

I *am* afraid of losing the Rochester family. But these feelings

I have for Felix are big, beautiful, resolute. *I want to risk it.* For him. For the possibility of an us.

I want to convince Felix to risk it, too.

Slowly. I want the idea to grow on him before I scare him away with directness.

"Hey," I say.

His head snaps up. "Hi."

"What are you musing about?"

"Stuff."

"How interesting."

He dashes his fingers through his hair. "Stuff about you."

I hitch a brow. "How fascinating."

He lets out a frustrated chuckle and throws his arms up. "Okay, truth—have we been distancing ourselves the last week?"

Yes. I've gone straight to my lonely house most days for two reasons. One, to wrestle with my nerve-wrecking decision. Two, Felix seemed to be wrestling with a decision of his own. His body language begged for space from me, and all my instincts told me to give it to him.

"A little bit—"

Felix's door flies open. April ducks her head into the car, braid flicking Felix's head.

"Are you coming in to help us make Christmas presents?"

Felix casts his eyes away from me. Okay, Felix. "Sorry, April, I—"

"Pleeeease? Don't you miss hanging out with us?"

"Of course I miss it. I miss it and you—"

"Not as much as we miss you," she says, pulling herself out the door. It thumps shut.

Felix watches her retreating figure.

"For the record," I say jovially. "April's wrong. When it comes to missing, I miss you guys more."

"And when it comes to missing us equally?"

He's asked me before and brushed it off as a joke, but it always tugs deeply in my gut.

He's not talking about the last week, he's talking about the year I wasn't here. He's talking about all the times we might be apart in the future.

I hum and withdraw the keys from the ignition. "I miss you all differently."

Felix lifts his head, eyes curious yet wary.

"I miss April and May for their curiosity and adventure and the way they copy me. I miss Tiffany's careful introspection and grace. I miss your mum—the one I looked up to as a kid. And I miss Roch." His name comes out on a sigh. I rub my chest. "I miss how close we were. Miss watching him dance. Miss lazy afternoons at the arcade. Miss sending him stupid gifs and receiving stupider ones back. Miss having someone who would have my back."

Felix blinks hard. "You miss him more than the others."

"*Differently*, Felix."

His face shutters until I can't read him. "Are things back to the way they were with you two?"

"I don't think they can go back. But we're both putting in effort; we're definitely mending."

Felix cracks open the car door. "I should really get inside." He starts to climb out.

I lunge over the console and grab him by the hips. "Not so fast, Felix." I hook my fingers into his belt loops and tug him back onto his seat. "You don't flee the car when I get to the part about missing *you*."

"I thought . . ." He mumbles the last bit. "You'd forgotten."

That kicks me in the gut. "Jesus, Felix. Forgetting anything about you is impossible."

His blue eyes hit mine.

"The same impossible it is to describe missing you."

Felix's face lights. He drops a small smile toward his lap.

"I've, um, got to help the twins make crystals from table salt. What are your plans?"

"Heating baked beans in my Dad's microwave."

He clears his throat, shifting nervously. "Mort, I have to help the twins make crystals from table salt, and you're . . .?"

My lips quirk. "Giving you a quick lesson on crystallization?"

He flashes me a relieved grin. "Thanks."

"Sodium chloride and sucrose crystals are hard to grow due to their solubility. They'll want to make crystals from copper sulfate—should be in their science kit. Concentration of the solution, temperature, pH levels, and presence of impurities will affect crystal growth. Add 100 grams of dry anhydrous copper sulfate to a glass jar, add a liter of water, heat until the sulfates dissolve, and leave in a cold room for a week. Voila, crystals."

"That sounds fascinating . . ."

I pause, eyeing Felix's glazed expression. "Summarize what I explained."

"Androgynous copper sulfate. Those words are loaded with important information."

"Anhydrous." I grin and rub my jaw. "What is this for?"

"They want to grow them for Mum's present. They think she'll love them."

There is an ache in the way Felix says this, and I feel it too.

"Right then." I look at Felix softly and repeat my explanation, simplifying it. When I'm done, I rock a quizzical brow. "You're still staring at me like I don't make sense."

He blushes. "Aren't I always staring at you?"

My grin might split my face. "What's happening behind those beautiful eyes, sunshine?"

He swallows, focusing on the science problem. "You've explained it twice, but . . ."

"But?" I wait for him to spit it out.

He swivels to face me. Deep emotion clouds his eyes but mischief glitters at the surface. "I like sitting in the front seat."

"Good."

"You like me sitting in the front seat."

"Like you wouldn't believe."

"I wouldn't want to climb into the back again . . ."

Ah, Felix. I chuckle briefly but sober to make a point: "You don't need to cajole me. Just ask what you want."

"I want you and those loaded words."

"Which ones? Anhydrous copper sulfate? Or that you have beautiful eyes?"

He gulps. "I, uh . . . the sciency ones."

"You sure?"

"Yes!"

I rub my jaw. "What do you want me to do?"

"Help me."

You bet, sunshine. "Shall I start by helping April and May make crystals?"

"I'll . . . heat baked beans for us afterwards."

I give him a dry look. "I'm not sure who's landing the better deal here."

"I'll throw in some tortilla chips."

"Add a movie, and I'll help you with the dishes."

He climbs out. "Then let's get in there and start throwing around more loaded words."

I intend to.

Chapter Twenty-Two

FELIX

MUM'S FOLDING LAUNDRY IN THE LIVING ROOM WHEN WE WALK inside. We exchange smiles, but the space between us bubbles with awkwardness and uncertainty. Just like with Mort and I last week.

I don't know what's wrong with me. Why can't I let the past go? Why do I drown myself in sepia-tinted memories of Roch and Mort instead of swimming in the unfiltered experiences of now?

Why did I want to cry at Mort's love-filled voice when he talked about missing him? Why do I focus on that even though Mort promised me I'm unforgettable? And said I have beautiful eyes?

And Mum. When did I stop hugging her hello?

I back up, accidentally bumping into a silently observing Mort. I whisk into the quiet kitchen.

April and May are already mucking around near the bridge.

The door to the living room shuts and Mort appears just left of my shoulder. His nearness sends prickles down my side.

I don't look at him. "You know what we need?"

"What's that?"

"Music."

Mort connects his phone to our Sonos speakers and plays Pax Polo.

"Might be the rock star I'm currently crushing on, but I need something else right now."

Mort twists around and leans against the counter I'm palming. He waves his phone. "Every playlist you need is right here."

"Pretty awesome playlists but not what I need. I need something slightly off tune, perfectly on beat. Something I haven't heard in forever."

His eyes clasp mine gently. "When are you going to talk frankly about how you feel?"

With Mum? Or . . . *With Mum.* "There hasn't been an ideal opportunity yet."

"If you need the girls out of the house, I can arrange that."

"I'll get around to it eventually."

"Or if you'd like moral support, I can help."

I shove away from the counter. "Why is this so important?"

"Your relationship with Dolores seems fragile. Like you don't know how to talk."

"We talk. We say good morning, good night. Ask about each other's day."

"*Really* talk, Felix."

Really talk. I don't remember the last time.

Mort clears his throat. "For *your* peace of mind—whatever that conversation looks like."

"She's been helping out with the girls and the house. She's making an effort. It's better enough."

"Enough?"

"Look, we talk, all right?"

"Okay."

"Back to dinner. I promised you nachos and beans."

"And a movie."

I open the pantry. Mort steps outside the back door and stops. "Felix?"

"Yes?"

"Slightly off tune, perfectly on beat? That was me and your mum singing Beatles songs after school every day."

Mort walks into the garden, and I close my stinging eyes and bury myself in the pantry.

The rest of the evening, I'm weirdly impatient and cranky. After making crystals and watching a movie, I snap at April and May. "Just go to bed without complaining for once in your freaking lives."

All eyes around the lounge whip to me scraping popcorn off the couch.

April and May give me sheepish looks while Mum hustles them out. They disappear and I try not to peer across the semi-darkened room at Mort and Tiffany, who had been haggling over the date of their next driving lesson.

Tiffany breaks the silence. "Well thank fuck. He's human after all."

I jerk my chin up. "What?"

Mort replies, "You're not *rolling the wave*."

Tiffany frowns, but I don't. I get it. *When Harry Met Sally*.

"The wave?" Tiffany asks.

"It's poignant," Mort says to her. To me. And he doesn't

mean the wave is poignant as in no matter how sad you are, you've got to keep rolling. He means this moment is poignant. Me. Not hiding behind a shrug and a smile. Not rolling the wave.

His eyes fuse to mine with intense understanding. I cross to him. My legs are shaky and my heart pounds. He doesn't look away or even twitch when I stop toe to toe before him. The TV screen is rolling credits.

I lift my chin. "Take it off."

"Uh, should I leave the room?" Tiffany asks, chuckling.

"Set your alarm. Your first driving lesson in The Groove is at six a.m."

She huffs but doesn't complain. Despite her resistance, she clearly wants to learn.

When her footsteps disappear, I refocus on Mort. We are alone, so I decide to expose my neck to him. "My bow tie. Take it off."

He runs a fingertip over my Adam's apple down to my collar. "Why?"

"There's nothing neat and together about me." I lick my dry lips. "I shouldn't be wrapped up in a bow."

"What are you saying?"

"I'm saying please take it off."

He fingers the knot while eyeing me, a challenge in his eyes. My pulse jack-rabbits. "But wearing bow ties makes you happy."

"I need to be happy without it first."

His breath hitches.

"Why do you want me untying you?"

"Because."

His finger dances between my shirt and throat, creating little puffs of air as he waits for me to continue.

Heat crawls up my neck—maybe he feels it. "I've admitted enough today, haven't I?"

Mort hums softly and picks open my knot.

I swallow. "I want to talk."

"With your mum?"

And with you. "Yes."

He pinches both ends of my tie and pulls me an inch forward. His words comb my upper lip. "I'm so fucking proud of you right now."

My cheeks are scalding. "And there'll be no more smiles."

"No more *fake* smiles."

To that, there's nothing to do but smile.

I MISS MORT WHEN I'M IN BED. THE MEMORY OF HIS GAZE penetrating mine makes my insides restless. I know it's unhealthy to imagine him as I stroke myself, but I do. I *always* do.

And my mind always skips to that one bitter-sexy memory. The one that makes my dick hard and my heart weep.

My free hand fishes under my thigh, one saliva-slickened finger probing my ass. I try to stick two fingers, three—it's messy. It's not enough.

Fantasies fill my mind. Questions. But I'm never wondering what a cock would feel like pounding into me. I'm wondering what *his* cock would feel like.

Strokes quicken, then slacken, quicken again. My body locks, my toes curl and my ass clenches around my fingers as I come.

I finger my scar through the come on my belly—a little tradition I started to remind myself that fantasies must remain fantasies. It usually sobers me quickly, but tonight I'm wondering if his come would feel different. Would be healing.

I knock my head back against my pillow and groan.

Well, crap.

I clean myself up in the bathroom and fling back into bed with my phone, swiping to my messages with Mort.

I type a message, then delete it. Three times. I'm about to put the phone down, when three dots start jumping—Mort is writing to me. But then he stops without sending.

I fall asleep to that mystery, and I wake to it too.

I'm still mulling over what Mort wanted to say when I climb into the back of the wagon at six the next morning.

I catch Mort studying me through the rearview mirror and my stomach lurches. I glance away.

"What?" I say to Mort, still feeling his eyes on me.

Mort pauses a moment and then says, "I'm not used to you sans bow tie."

"I'm not used to you with bed hair."

He runs a hand through it. "Didn't sleep much. Misplaced my cap."

"You sure you want to take this lesson?"

He smirks. "Who doesn't want to wake up at six in the morning on their holiday?"

"It slipped out last night. I was in a decision-making mood."

"I liked it."

"Anyway," I roll my shoulders. "The parking lots are empty now, so . . ."

"We going where I taught you?"

"Outside The Warehouse, yeah."

Mort claps his hands with a *let's do this* smack. He peeks over his seat. "No backseat drivers."

I scowl playfully and roam my fingers lovingly over the vinyl seat. "Feels familiar back here. I forgot how much I like it."

Mort clarifies, bemused. "Minimal backseat driver instructing."

I wink. "You got it."

Air washes into the car and Tiffany piles into the passenger seat clutching bright yellow L plates. I lean between the seats, pinch one from her, and stick it in the back window.

"What a beautiful morning for a driving lesson," Mort says to Tiffany.

"It's a beautiful morning," she grumbles.

Mort drives us to an empty parking lot outside The Warehouse, shuts off the car, and turns to Tiffany. "Want to hop in the driver's seat?"

"Not really, no."

"Why not?"

"Better view from this side."

"Okay, honey," Mort says warmly, and my heart melts.

Tiffany tightens her hair tie. "Have you ever been in a car accident?" she asks Mort.

"Years ago. Minor collision. The other driver was at fault."

"Were you hurt?" Tiffany and I ask at the same time.

I grip both front seats, jamming myself against the console as I inspect Mort for scars I might have missed.

Mort's gaze flickers between Tiffany and me, resting on me. "I had a stiff shoulder for a month. Nothing else."

I want to rip off his T-shirt and double check for myself.

Tiffany shoves me back an inch and continues quizzing Mort. "Ever had a car break down on you?"

"No, but I schedule regular car maintenance checks."

"So you wouldn't know what to do if The Groove suddenly stopped working?"

"I'd handle it."

Tiffany narrows her eyes. "What would you do?"

Mort grins. "Do I need a lawyer?"

"I'm judge and jury here," she says.

"You'd make a good one."

"I'll consider studying law. Have you ever experienced a seatbelt malfunction?"

I gently tug Tiffany's ponytail through the gap in the head rest. "There are scissors under the seat for emergencies. He's good at this, Tiffany. Mort taught me how to drive."

Mort shakes his head. "Obviously didn't spend enough time on speeding limits and stop signs." He focuses on Tiffany. "I will do that with you though. Swap seats?"

"Um . . ."

"We'll take it one step at a time. Like a dance."

She blinks at him. "A dance?"

"Dancing makes you feel good, secure, confident. So think of this as a waltz, yeah?"

"How?"

Mort steps out of the car and rounds to Tiffany's side. "First, you'll lead."

Tiffany eyes his offered hand, pauses a beat, then grasps it.

I'm so excited for Tiffany, I can barely sit still. Mort takes her place in the passenger seat and Tiffany slides behind the wheel with a nervous, "Now what?"

"Music of course." Mort plays soft instrumental music and Tiffany visibly relaxes.

"Good call, Mort," I say. "It's like you're a teacher or something."

He rolls his eyes.

"Set the seat so you're comfortable. Think of this as your driving posture."

She aligns her feet and mirrors. "Okay, okay, okay."

"Let's look at your footwork now."

Tiffany eyes the pedals. "I wish this were an automatic."

I quote Mort from our first lesson together: "Learn to drive a manual and you can drive anything."

Mort walks Tiffany through the steps to shift gears.

And we are moving. About two miles an hour. "You compare this to a waltz?" Tiffany shrieks. "This is a salsa. With multiple spins."

She glides through the parking lot in first gear, chanting, "Oh my God. Oh my God. Felix?"

I lean forward. "Yes?"

"I'm so making you learn a salsa."

Mort's eyes ping to mine. "Sounds great to me," he says, the instant I say, "What have I ever done to you, Tiff?"

Tiffany is back to her "oh my God" chant as she makes a wide bend. "Did you freak out when you started driving, Felix?"

Mort barks out a laugh. "His first lesson. This is nothing on Felix's *fuck-me* mantra."

Tiffany gasps. "He rarely says fuck."

"Only when I'm scared," I say. "Or exhilarated."

"Which I guess isn't often," Tiffany says.

"I assure you," Mort chimes, "Felix made up for it that day."

She giggles. "What other stories do you have?"

"Three lessons in, Felix clicked. He became one with the car and—actually, I decided at that moment— alongside my science major—I wanted to teach." Mort's lips twist up, eyes glassy like he's lost in the memory. "The elation on his face, realizing he could do it . . . knowing I helped." I shut my eyes briefly on the current charging through me. "It was an incredible feeling."

So is this one. My voice strangles. "You became a teacher because of me?"

"I realized my true calling because of you."

I stare at his profile, fingers locked on the front seats.

"More stories," Tiffany pleads.

I jerk my attention to her, then jabber on about the time Mort forgot to put the handbrake on while he was paying for gas. I was studying for exams in the passenger seat and didn't realize the car was rolling out of the station until I was on the road.

"Not the best story. Considering."

I throw Mort a sheepish shrug. "Funny though."

Mort switches the music to the songs we used to practice our waltz. "Some of my favorite memories are taking car trips with your brothers and overnighting in the back."

"What's your best memory in The Groove?" Tiffany asks, stealing from my lips.

"I, uh . . . too many to choose from." I don't believe him. Maybe there are many to choose from, but Mort knows his favorite. So many mysteries today.

"What's yours, Felix?"

I refocus. My favorite moment in the wagon. "It was before I learned to drive."

Mort's glittering eyes hit mine in a silent laugh. He knows the one. "It's the reason I decided to teach you."

I can't look away. "I stole his car keys and stuttered out the drive."

We bounce over a speed bump. "Why'd you steal his keys?"

"We were at this party a few blocks away and he was drunk. I thought I could drive him home. I think the *fuck-me* mantra was born there. I was laughing so hard, I peed myself."

"Never been that drunk," Mort says. "But since Felix had no hesitance to dive into my pocket and grab my keys, I thought I should teach him to do it right. The driving part."

The car stalls, and Tiffany decides she's done enough driving for today. Mort starts to encourage her to do a little more, but he accepts her wish. Patient and kind.

When they change seats again, Mort catches my eye in the mirror. "You okay, Felix?"

What, because I look like I've baked in the sun for a year? "You really remember the pocket bit?" I squawk.

A dark smile plows into me. "Vividly."

~

"VIVIDLY?" WE'RE PARKED OUTSIDE OUR PLACE, WATCHING Tiffany hike up the path. "What was that?"

"Me recalling a memory," Mort says.

"Yes, but." I kick off my shoes, weasel between the seats, and flop into the front, socked feet on the console. I rest one foot at his hip and wedge the other one under his armpit. "How many shared memories do you recall in that detail?"

He snatches my tickling foot and stills it against him. "Want me to tally it up for you?"

"Ballpark."

"If that was the third time you gave me a hard-on . . . then there was the time in the bush you tripped over a tree root and landed us in the dirt . . . and that other time in the stream . . ." He thumbs the backs of my toes as he lures me closer with his sparkling eyes. "All of them."

I swallow. "All of them?"

"Wait." He rubs my toes again and nods. "Yes. All of them."

"You also remember the time I wrote on the back of bushman's toilet paper and—"

"—sent me notes sailing downstream, yeah."

"And when—"

"That, too."

"You don't even know what I was going to say."

Mort swivels toward me and sets my feet on his lap. "But I know the memory."

The heat simmering from his thigh to my heels steals my thoughts. Nodding proves to be an achievement. "Go on then."

He starts massaging my feet—and I might just call it a good life and die right now.

"When you picked up Roch and me from the airport after our first semester at uni, and Roch was sick, and we had to haul him with our luggage and wheel him to the wagon."

"Nope."

"At the glowworm cave, lying on a blanket, the roof glittering. Roch was trying to persuade Lauren to come in, but she was too freaked out. It ended up only us for the night."

"Until Coop and Jace stumbled over us in a fit of passion . . . But, that wasn't the memory I was thinking of."

"It's a nice one though. The part where we talked all night."

"Yes," I say on a wistful breath.

He runs a blunt fingernail along the arch of my foot to the ball. "The time my ex-boyfriend dumped me over a text at Christmas. You ran up to me at the tree and told me he wasn't worth a single gloomy thought." Mort fuses our gazes together. "You said, 'Real love will feel like sunshine'."

Oh. I . . . um . . . yes. I said that.

I'd forgotten. Not the stupid ex part, but my words. My voice shakes. "Wow. You remember. All of them."

We stare heatedly at each other. I am definitely going to combust. I need a cold shower. A bath of ice. Burial under Fox Glacier.

"You started writing to me last night and stopped." And I jump right to that.

His brows jump. "So did you."

Ah, so we'd both been staring at the bouncing dots, wondering what he wasn't saying.

"I couldn't sleep," I say.

"Neither could I."

April and May burst out the front door, waving go-cart designs, aiming for us.

Mort tucks my feet onto my seat. I crack open the door. "Did I really give you hard-ons?"

A smile pinches his lips. "Mmm."

"Mmm?"

"Well." We climb out the car and he shoots me a tingly look over the roof. "I wouldn't be so quick to use past tense."

Chapter Twenty-Three

MORT

The following week—the week before Christmas—is a rush of shopping, work parties, and menu prep. No chance to steal a moment alone with Felix. Probably unlikely the next few days either.

But damn, I need one.

I slide a tray of Christmas mince pies into the oven and give Dolores firm instructions for removal. She throws me a half-hearted thumbs-up over a cookbook. I bound upstairs.

Felix is pulling folded scarves from his closet. He's wearing nothing but a tight pair of boxer shorts and wet hair. His ivory skin is smooth and lean muscle flexes as he plants the scarves on the bed and swivels back for a handful of shirts.

"Felix?"

He whisks around and clutches the shirts against his naked torso. "Hi."

Piles of clothes staple the floor. Open boxes sit on his desk and dresser. Shirts and jackets are slung over the bed. "Are you moving out?"

"Ha! That'd be the day." He turns away and slinks into a shirt. He never used to care when I saw him shirtless, and I'll forever curse myself for leaving. I can't see his scar, but it stretches there, between us.

He resumes emptying his closet in fast, aggravated movements. "Maybe I'll move when the twins start high school. Or if Mum improves. It would be nice, my own place. But I'd want to be close—and it'd have to be big enough to start my own family. Three fostered children would be perfect." He tosses clothes onto his bed and twists toward me. "But I'm beginning to suspect . . . maybe not."

I sag against the doorframe, ploughed with tender images of Felix and me raising kids. Starting our own family. "Not the answer I was expecting." I clear the frog in my throat. "But I like what you're saying under the frustration."

He grimaces, scoping out the mess in his room.

"Why would you think you couldn't handle it?"

He throws his hands up. "If I can't keep track of where I hide Christmas gifts, how will I keep track of kids who hide for fun?"

Ah. "You've misplaced some gifts?"

"And it's Christmas Eve." He shoves aside some shirts and slumps onto his bed. "How long until tomorrow?"

"Fourteen hours."

He winces, glaring at the floor. "I might just make it in time."

I pick my way into the room. "Which gifts are you searching for?"

"Bow ties with periodic-table print, and a dance tote bag."

"I assume you had them—"

"—somewhere in this room, yes."

I smile at his cute exasperation. "I was going to say together."

He throws himself back over his shirts. "It would be enough to misplace one gift. Not *all* the gifts!"

I inspect his closet. Just one box left—

"Don't look in there." The cupboard door shuts. A flushed Felix slides in front of me, reaching to close the other door.

I don't tell him it's too late. I saw his box of dildos and—more incriminating—Roch's senior yearbook. *My* yearbook. The one with me celebrating on the soccer pitch after winning a game, on my knees, shirt swinging around my head.

I stare at his eyes. Hand gripping the door, he darts his tongue over his lips.

"Let me help you out," I say.

His breath catches and his gaze darts to my lips. "With what?"

I groan internally. Felix is killing me. We need more time just the two of us. "Finding your gifts."

"Of course. Yes!" He checks the latch is closed and gestures at me to inspect his desk.

I thoroughly investigate the drawers.

Felix checks his trunk. "I suppose all your gifts are sorted and wrapped already?"

"Well."

He grumbles.

I glance at him, and he glances away—like a game of tag. I want to laugh. I bloody well want to kiss the bejesus out of him.

"What?" Felix says when it happens again.

I perch on his desk and fold my arms. "Three foster children?"

"Yes."

"You're really planning this?"

"Not so much planning as dreaming."

"Why three?"

"So we can all fit in one car."

I make a quick, heart-thumping calculation. "There is a partner in this plan." Not a question. *Please, me.*

"Dream. Yes. Three kids is a lot to handle on your own."

"But you do it on your own."

He settles his bright blue eyes on me. "I wasn't much good at it before you came back."

I grip the desk. "Felix . . ."

He rubs his nape. "Maybe I accidentally threw them out?" He double-checks his closet. "Where are they?"

The doorbell chimes, and Felix jumps. "Roch and Lauren."

"Dolores can answer."

"She might not, though. Check?"

Roch and Lauren are in the kitchen peering into the oven when I get downstairs.

We embrace, and Roch starts right in after an elbow in the ribs from Lauren. "Right. About our wedding invite . . . are you accepting?"

Yes. Except . . . "Sort of."

"If you don't agree now, you'll miss out on a spot at table two and you'll be squeezed in last minute at table ten—with all the kids."

I wince. "Okay."

"Okay? They're not as cool as ours."

I chuckle. "I'll manage." But maybe—*maybe*—I won't have to.

The twins steal Lauren away. Roch races up the stairs to Felix for an update on the family; I trail behind.

Roch saunters into the room. "There's my Felix."

Felix starts to smile—looks at me—and drops it. "Careful where you step."

"Mort says you're searching for misplaced gifts. I'm great at finding lost things."

"It's a maze in here, maybe better if you don't help."

Roch grins. "It'll be fine. I'm not the clumsy one."

Felix snaps his gaze to me at my chuckle. I hide my grin behind a fist and clear my throat. "Three guys a charm, right?"

Felix stares at his feet. "I think the saying is three's a crowd."

Roch snaps his fingers. "On the topic of crowds, sorta. It's Christmas. You bringing a plus-one to my wedding?"

Felix's shoulders droop.

"Yes, he is," I say.

"I am?"

"Yep."

His frown wobbles. "You seem certain."

"*Hopeful.*"

Roch navigates to Felix and stands in front of him, fingering his bow tie-less collar. "Okay, you and your date will sit at our table."

Felix straightens. "Your table?"

"I was hoping you'd be my best man?"

"Because I can sit anywh—what did you say?"

"You'll have to stand next to me during vows, too."

"Best man?"

Roch's smile widens. The brotherly love beats hard between them. "Best man."

"What are my other responsibilities?"

"I don't want a bachelor party so . . . moral support and helping me find the perfect bow tie."

A warm smile touches Felix's face. "I just *might* be able to help there." His smile fades. "Are you sure you want me?"

I prop my back against the wall, thumbs loose in my shorts. "Roch asked if you'd say yes, and I think you're the perfect choice."

Roch pulls Felix into a hug. "I want roles for all my siblings. April and May, flower girls. They've already asked if they can dye the petals."

"And Tiffany?"

"Still planning something for her."

An idea forms and I grin. The wedding is not for two months. Perfect. "I know exactly what Tiffany can do."

Roch lifts a puzzled brow. "What?"

I tell them. Felix's smile brightens, and Roch nods. "Perfect. Now tell me," he looks at Felix, "how are your dancing lessons coming along?"

He playfully shoves Roch. "Get out of here. I've got gifts to find."

"Have you checked under your bed?"

Felix pales slightly and drops to his knees. He stares long and hard into the dark space under the bed. He calmly pulls back. "Nope. Absolutely not under the bed."

Lauren's call immediately diverts Roch's attention. I wait until he's out of sight before I crawl to Felix's bed and pull out his missing gifts. "Come downstairs for Christmas mince pies."

He looks at the bag, and curses. "You see right through me."

I laugh. "I like what I see."

His face pales. "Oh crap. You know what's in the closet, don't you?"

Our gazes shoot to the mirrored door that reflects us. He groans. "You know I . . . think of you."

"I'm guessing."

He claps a hand on his nape. "I suppose that can't come as much of a surprise."

No. I've suspected as much before. But will it surprise him that I do the same?

God, I wish Roch and the rest of the family weren't just downstairs.

"I'm . . . uh, sorry."

I drop the bag on his bed and tip his chin up with my finger. "Don't be."

~

CHRISTMAS EVE AND CHRISTMAS DAY FLY BY WITH THE USUAL barbecue shenanigans.

The approach of New Year's Eve has the twins and I working hard on their go-karts.

I carry the tools to the back yard and settle them next to the picnic table lined with car parts. Daylight spits blindingly off the metal. "Will we ever do things together that don't include building these go-karts?" I tease.

April glances at me sternly over the top of her detailed designs. "I think you're forgetting all the weekends we chase you around the soccer pitch."

I brace my hands on my hips and survey the equipment. "Ah, your illegal tackles. Such fun."

May giggles from the end of the table, feet swinging. "I'm sorry, Mort, but you are expected to guide us through each step." She picks up the portable welding clamp and inspects it.

April pinches it off her. "Possibly take over a couple, too. Although . . ."

Too much glee in her expression. "Put that down. You're absolutely right. I'm not going anywhere."

Not that I ever intended to.

A door slams, and Felix exuberantly strides towards us. He's wearing the short-sleeve shirt I bought him for Christmas, navy shorts, and his Chucks. "I'm here! Finally, I know. I was dealing with a case of self-persuasion. In that I had to persuade myself to help build stuff."

The twins and I share a baffled look. Felix has never volunteered his help, and neither have we asked him to.

"Glad to see you won the battle?" April says tentatively.

Felix frowns at the equipment. "I'd have said *lost*, technically."

His sneaky glance at me puts my synapses on alert and

tingles my gaydar. He's not here for the go-karts. He's here for me. The question is: is he aware of that?

Is he starting to see us for what we could be?

I swallow eager hopefulness—and nearly choke when I catch Felix looking.

He picks up a foot-long steel pipe and strokes his hand up and down it. "What does this do?"

April and May share an immature snicker, and I step close to Felix, amused. "This is a PG-rated afternoon, Felix. Either take the pipe to your room or stop fondling it."

His hand freezes and he stares at the pipe—and the very explicit way he's holding it. He drops it to his side and whispers back, "Is taking it back to my room an actual option?"

God, he's flirting with me.

Damn. I like it.

I wish I could see inside his head. Wish I could read the narrative he's telling himself as to why he came out here. Wish I had him alone, but . . . the twins. I need to focus on the task at hand.

I clap my hands. "Let's get started, then. April, May, you know where we're at. As for your brother, I have the perfect role for him."

The girls look quizzically between us. "Nothing requiring any co-ordination, I hope?"

Felix gives May an affronted look before turning to me. "She has a great point. So where do you want me? Holding something down while you saw? Passing you the tools?"

"Taking photos." I pat him on the back. "Document this stage of go-kart assembly."

"Thank God. I'm not sure me or my phone could figure out the names of all these bits. Wow, there are lots of bits. How many go-karts are you making?"

I laugh. "Just the two."

Felix whips out his phone. "Say cheese."

April smiles perfunctorily. "Cheese. Now, let's fit the floor, then sort out the brakes."

I nod. "Sounds good."

"Sounds complicated," Felix says, amazed.

He takes more pictures as we work, but his phone is mostly angled in my direction. Focusing on the go-karts suddenly becomes difficult.

When Felix unabashedly steps over the go-kart to get a close-up of me, I can't hold back. "How're you doing, sunshine?"

His blue eyes dance. "This is more fun than I thought."

I bite down a chuckle and raise a challenging brow. "You know, there's a lot more to shoot than me and my tools."

Felix blushes behind his phone and I suck in a breath, awaiting his reply.

"You're, um . . . right," he says, spinning around too quickly. He doesn't steer his lens my way again.

Once we've welded the floor in and fixed the brakes in place, the twins are ready for the next step, and I'm ready for alone time with Felix. I catch his eye. "Still having fun?"

Felix jumps, and flushes. He gives a bored shrug that I don't believe for a second. "We have wildly different ideas of fun."

I clean my hands on a rag. "No one forced you out here, Felix."

"No, I . . . hmm." His expression folds into contemplation.

I want to fold him in my arms and whisper consolations. But the twins are tugging on my arm. "The steering arms, yes. We'll get to that next." Felix stares into space, while looking in my direction. I wave his favorite steel pipe for attention. "How are the photos looking?"

"Good. Good. Great. The afternoon lighting—it's fantastic."

I set down the pipe. "Pass your phone."

He eyes me suspiciously but thrusts it toward me. "Why?"

I swipe to the camera. "It's fantastic lighting." I take a few snapshots of Felix and hand it over. "Update your profile pic."

He shakes his head, smirking. "You're so weird about that."

"Not weird. I like to see you."

"You see me every day."

I step closer and his gaze flickers. "It's not enough."

May leaps between us for a steering wheel. "When will our karts be ready to test drive?"

"Next year."

"Next *year*?"

"That's only three days away."

Dolores calls out to us, announcing Roch's arrival with a PlayStation. The twins stop griping about the steering wheels and try to scamper inside, dragging Felix with them, but I call them back to clean up.

Thirty minutes later, I'm helping Roch set up the PlayStation.

Tiffany approaches me crouched at the TV. She playfully punched my shoulder during our fourth driving lesson this morning, so I'm positive that the air between us is warming.

"Tiffany?"

She fumbles with her cell phone. "I have a favor to ask."

I straighten. "Name it."

"Arjun is having a party tonight and wouldyoudrivemethere?"

Felix, flung lengthwise on the couch, watches us curiously. His hair sweeps over one eye as he lazily scratches his exposed navel. I rip my gaze back to Tiffany. "You bet."

Tiffany's smile is rewarding, but not as rewarding as Felix's. That smile yo-yo's my gut.

Roch looks like he wants to say something but can't spit it out.

"What's going on, Roch?"

He jerks his head away and laughs stiffly. "What about a game of Dance Dance Revolution? Felix says he beat my old score at the arcade."

I drop the cable. Felix said *what* now?

Behind Roch, Felix swings his legs to the floor. His eyes widen, caught in a lie.

I attach the cable to the TV. "Is that right? Well, let me set the record straight." Felix cringes in anticipation. I school my expression. "He's fibbing." His shoulders deflate. I lean toward Roch and add, "He also beat mine."

Relief swamps over Felix and he mouths, "What the hell?"

I flash a secret smile and make his lips tick up.

Roch flops next to Felix on the couch and slings an arm around him. "Really, Felix? There's a dancer in you after all?"

Felix thumps his forehead against Roch's shoulder.

Roch continues, "This should be a fun afternoon, then."

"Felix can't play today," I say swiftly. "He hurt his ankle during our dance session last night."

A lie, but Tiffany's interest in our conversation piques.

"Shame," Roch says. "I can't wait to check out your arcade score though."

Ah, shit.

Chapter Twenty-Four

FELIX

After hours playing video games, Mort brings fish 'n' chips for dinner.

He unwraps the massive bundle and I hover around the china cabinet, eyeing the wine rack. I've been a lump of shivery goosebumps being in the same room with Mort the last few days.

Because despite the whole family's presence, it feels as if it's just the two of us.

"Gonna sit down, sunshine?"

"I'm . . . going to grab the Merlot."

Roch stops me at the doorway, hauling me toward the table. "A prime case of never judging a book by its cover. He appears so cultured, but underneath"—he traces my button-down and smooths it, chuckling. "Fish 'n' chips and wine."

Mort slants a reproachful look at Roch but suppresses his amusement. "Rich coming from you, hot sauce."

Roch bubbles out a laugh. "Hear that, Felix? We could be twins."

"No," Mort says too quickly, startling Roch into a puzzled look.

Mort's gaze jerks between the two of us and settles on the dinner at the table. "You're different."

"Really?" Roch says. "Let's hear it, then. What makes me better?"

"Different. Not better," Mort says in a teacher voice. "Let's eat."

Nervously, I draw out a chair and sit.

"Don't smother all the chips with hot sauce," Mort growls at Roch, shaking his head.

"I'm not smothering all the chips. Just most of them."

Mort dives into the food, creating a valley of oil-stained paper through the fries.

"Wow," Roch says over a fry, "you haven't been this protective of food since you were sixteen."

Mort side-eyes Roch. "I had a healthy appetite."

"You had an appetite. Whether it could be called *healthy* . . ."

They share a melancholic smile. I remind myself this is why these weird shivery feelings have to go. I crash a fry against my teeth. I try again, popping it into my mouth.

Mort twists the glossy paper, swiveling the mound of fish 'n' chips until the sauce-less area sits before me.

Thoughtfulness doesn't mean I'm the love of Mort's life.

No matter how often the butterflies and the memory of Mort's "don't be" make me think otherwise.

I excuse myself to the kitchen and pour a healthy glass of Merlot. The light above the oven casts a bright circle over the wedge of kitchen island where I stand.

Conversation bubbles in the next room. I find solace at the end of my first glass.

A shadow at the cracked door precedes Mum's entrance. The click of the latch snuffs out Roch's and Mort's voices.

I take a long sip, eyeing her over the rim.

She's wearing a green dress and her cheeks are flushed. It's the healthiest I've seen her look in months. Of course, as Roch so wisely pointed out, looks can be deceiving.

She picks up a candle surrounded by homemade crystals that April and May gave her for Christmas and lights a flame.

"It's like a year ago, all over again," she murmurs.

"Sorry?"

"Roch and Mort, chummy together." She sets the crystal candle down. "You, watching them like a disqualified dancer at the ballroom championships."

That is . . . painfully accurate.

She steps forward and rubs my arm. "Just forget about him, Felix."

I swirl the contents of my glass and speak softly. "Are you saying this for my sake? Or your own?"

Mum drops her arm and a whiff of her perfume billows over me. Guilt races over her made-up face, and the lines around her mouth deepen.

"I know you hate that Mort's gay." I hold her gaze. "Will you send me away, too? Because I look at him? Because I wish he'd look at me too? Because I wish one day, a man will?"

I feel surprisingly steady. Maybe Mort has sufficiently numbed my nerves.

Maybe downing the Merlot helped.

"I've known Mort was gay since high school," I say. "You see how I look at him. Surely you saw how he looked at Roch."

I continue, anger seeping into my voice. "When did you start to hate it? When he said the words to you last year? When you couldn't deny it any longer? When did Mort turn from son to son-of-the-devil?"

"It's not like that."

"How is it, then?"

"I want to accept you, I do. I just . . . I thought I was dying." She takes a deep breath. "I prayed so hard to live. Every day, every other minute."

A horrible fist squeezes my stomach, penetrating the numbness. I barely get the words out. "To the same God you ran away from at fifteen?"

Her voice is small. "Maybe your father left and I got sick as punishment."

I don't know what to say. I can't grapple with how she feels, but she's not the only one who prays for things to be different.

"You don't know what it's like, staring at death, Felix. It's vulnerable. Frightening. Praying kept me alive."

I rest my glass on the island and take her hands. "No, Mum. That was me."

She swipes a tear trickling down her cheek. "I love you, Felix. I love you so much. I love all of you."

I kiss her forehead. "Love is April and May making you bioluminescent pearl necklaces, dressing up for Halloween, spending weeks growing crystals because they want you to be happy. Love is Tiffany telling you she won't watch movies until you change your medication—and then watching every Brené Brown feature with you online. Love is Mort." My voice cracks. "Mort forgiving you, rooting for you, even though you told him he wasn't worthy of being in our family. Love is me, shaking as I tell you this. 'I love yous' are just words. I want my mum back."

Limbs like jelly, I leave her standing in the kitchen next to her flickering candle.

I grab the keys to the wagon and lock myself inside it.

It's barely six o'clock and summer sun bathes the front seats, warm against my cool skin.

I feel empty and raw, and I want to be anywhere but here.

I curse my suspended driver's license and hit the steering wheel, accidentally hitting the horn.

My phone dings.

Mort: Are you in The Groove?

Me: Ha! I'm certainly not in the groove.

I regret it the second I send it.

Regret it more when Mort knocks on my window.

"Open up, Felix."

Laughter bubbles out of me. Because . . . because . . . opening up is exactly what I did. And what I still have to do. And what I find incredibly difficult.

Chapter Twenty-Five

MORT

Felix climbs into the passenger seat. I slide onto the warm vinyl and eye him. He's looking everywhere but at me, and I want to know what's wrong.

I start to ask, but he cuts over me. "Drive?"

I fish out the keys with Felix's Christmas gift dangling from them: a miniature-wagon keyring and a spare set of keys for the Rochester house. More sentimental than a damn shirt, but I couldn't very well give him the bow tie I'd carved out of wood. Not when he wasn't ready for it.

"Where to?"

"Somewhere over the rainbow."

I drive, and Felix urges me farther and farther out of the city. We're in the Wairarapa when the sun starts to settle on the horizon.

"Keep driving," he says, over Pax Polo's voice through the speakers.

I fork toward Castle Point, driving along windy backroads. The countryside glows like an emerald, and I chase the sinking sun.

I take a narrow dirt path, stray gravel pinging against the car. Sheep and goats crowd surrounding farms. A rooster flies onto a wooden fence, ruffling his feathers. Potholes slow me down, and ten minutes later, a dead end forces me back.

My phone buzzes. Felix eyes my pocket.

"Take my phone out?" I ask, cocking my hips for his access.

His breath hitches and his fingers slide over my upper thigh as he pulls out my phone.

I could have pulled it out myself, but I wanted to see Felix's eyes light up. And for a moment, they dance with surprise followed by gentle apprehension and a flood of desire.

My smile vanishes as Felix reads the message on my screen and curses. "We need to get back. Tiffany wants to know where we are."

Arjun's party. Shit.

She'd wanted to leave at eight. It's already quarter past.

We trundle around a bend and I step on the brakes.

A herd of sheep blocks the road. No farmer in sight.

Felix scrubs his eyes. "I'm not actually seeing this."

Gold and green wings flap, and a rooster lands on our hood. Huh. That was something.

Felix turns off Pax Polo, and faint bleating replaces the rock star.

"Mort!" Felix says.

I wince. "Yeah."

"What is happening?"

"I believe," I say with a drum roll against the wheel, "we're being cock-blocked."

Startled laughter morphs into a growl. "How are you having fun? Tiffany needs us."

"I feel bad about that."

"I should never have told you to keep driving." He slides his fingers through his hair and grips the ends.

"Roch is still at home, I'm sure he'll take her."

"Yes, but." Felix stares at the rooster. "She asked *you*, you know?"

It meant something. An acknowledgement of our relationship. "I know."

"We'll beg her forgiveness when she's back."

"I'm stopping you there, sunshine. I hear you feel like we're letting Tiffany down."

"Because we are."

I lean against the headrest. "She wanted something from me tonight and so did you. We're not surrounded by sheep in the Wairarapa for the fun of it. You need a break from home, and I need to give you one." I sigh. "Yeah, I'm letting Tiffany down. But when it comes to choosing who should get help first?" I hook his gaze. "It's going to be you."

His chest expands. "Me?"

"Every. Single. Time." I gesture to my phone he's gripping and give him the unlock key. "Call Tiffany and we'll apologize for not helping today, and for not being there tomorrow."

"Tomorrow? What do you mean?" He surveys the farm life surrounding us. "We'll be cock-blocked all night?"

I shift into first gear, slowly rolling forward. The rooster flies off the car. "Not if I can help it."

"I have work tomorrow."

"You have a night out with me tonight."

He gulps and stares out the windshield. "So, once you've navigated through these dozen sheep, we'll—"

"Dozen? There are fifty, at least. And when we retell this story, there'll be a hundred."

"Excuse me. Once we navigate through forty million sheep, we'll . . ."

"Better. We'll head to the best place on Earth." Felix sucks on his lips. I smirk at him. "Not my bed, Felix."

"Holy crap. Stop reading my depraved mind."

I laugh. "Call Tiff."

"Take my hand, Felix."

We're standing at the lighthouse on Castle Point. Waves lash at the rocks, and wind tunnels around us. The ocean is wild, and the brilliant beam of light is almost blinding.

Felix blinks at my outstretched hand.

"I want to dance with you."

He looks around. Another couple is huddled behind us. "Tiff said for us to have *fun,* Mort."

I laugh. "You don't want to dance with me?"

He swallows. "No, I do."

He slides his hand into mine and I grasp it. "This isn't all about fun, Felix. It's also about being close." I walk him to the middle of the clearing, settle his hand on my shoulder, and slide an arm around his back. I steer him into a waltz. He folds with me, his clean, soapy scent tickling my nose. "So, this evening at home . . ."

Felix slides closer, arm hooking my nape as if he plans to curl into me. He stops himself and gazes toward the ocean. "Can we forget about this evening?"

"Nope, but we can come back to it."

I shorten our steps, his body intimately close to mine.

His voice shakes. "What's your favorite memory in The Groove?"

"What sent your mind there?"

"The need to change subject, quick. Roll with it."

I run my fingers between his shoulder blades, up and down. It's cooler at the ocean and we're both in short sleeves.

"Also," he adds, "You refused to tell Tiffany, and I can't stop wondering why."

We dance for a beat, and I improvise a turn. Felix laughs, and I pull him close again. "I didn't tell her, because that declaration wasn't meant for her ears."

"Declaration?"

We're slow dancing not waltzing now, though we maintain a triple-count beat. "Every time I'm in The Groove with you is my favorite memory. Each time is better than the last. Which makes tonight's the best."

"Oh." He buries his head against my neck. "Really?"

"Really."

His breath skates down my throat before he pulls back, meeting my eye. "I thought I was supposed to be leading?"

"It felt like you wanted me to lead this time. Do you want to swap?"

"No. I want you to lead this. All of it."

I improvise another twirl and Felix growls. "Maybe without making me dizzier than I already am."

God, Felix makes me laugh. "We're sleeping together tonight."

"What did I *just* tell you?"

"Must have forgotten." I bump his nose with mine. "I'm a bit dizzy myself."

Felix rolls his shoulders and changes his grip on my fingers. His tongue darts nervously over his bottom lip. "You mean we're crashing in the back of The Groove tonight."

"We're crashing in the back of The Groove."

His voice hops and he pulls back. "I remember the last time we did that. Roch almost broke my nose flailing about."

I step closer. "Roch will not be between us."

Felix looks away uneasily.

"Since it's our first sleepover," I continue, "we need to make some rules."

"Rules. Sure. I'll stay on one side of the wagon and you, the other."

I laugh humorlessly. Not happening, sunshine. "*I'm* the chauffeur. I make the rules."

"What?" Felix shakes his head. "No way. I'm the owner."

I stop dancing and curl a fist. "Rock, paper, scissors. Best of three."

I knock Felix out in the second round—but I suspect he isn't trying too hard.

We dance, his palm growing clammy against mine.

"Here are the rules," I say at his ear. "We sleep together in the most comfortable way possible. If you crave crackers, spread crumbs wherever you want. If you need to take a leak, wake me so I can make sure you return to the wagon safely. If you want to whisper secrets into my ear all night, go ahead. And if you throw your limbs over mine? If your front clamps against my chest? If your morning wood pushes up against mine? So be it."

His shiver sinks into me.

"I don't want either of us to feel embarrassed or uncertain. Tonight, we're open. We're real. We're us."

Felix's lips comb over the cleft in my chin. "That sounds . . . yes."

I push back a lock of his hair. His blue eyes behold mine with raw intensity. "What happened this evening, Felix?"

He swallows. "I talked to Mum. *Talked* to her."

"How does that make you feel?"

"Kind of ill. Kind of relieved. Kind of hopeful." He tells me every word they shared, until he's trembling in my arms. "I told her I wanted my mum back. During the drive out here, I kept asking myself what does that look like? And do you know what image I kept circling back to?"

"Share it with me?"

"You and her singing "Yesterday." Her embracing you. Her

fondly stealing your cap off your head for dinner time." Felix's eyes lift to mine. "I kept asking myself, why don't the images include Roch or me or the girls, and it's because . . . she *has* been trying with us lately. She's been offering to help more. She's working on all of her relationships, except yours."

I stop waltzing. "We're getting there too, Felix."

He shakes his head. "Not enough. I need her to apologize to you, Mort. I need her to love you. Because you're my family too."

I'm slammed with an incredible ache, beautiful and breathless. The fragile feeling runs deep.

I'm afraid to speak in case I break it.

I thread our fingers together and lead the way to the car.

Felix says nothing about our laced fingers, but he stares at our hands most of the hike back.

I let go at the wagon and prepare the back for sleeping. The carpeting is padded for trips like these, and there are always blankets in The Groove.

Felix rests against the car, staring toward the distant lighthouse.

I slip beside him, arms pressing, knuckles bumping. In profile, Felix's nose tips up and his lips curve softly, gently parted. His cool arm rests against mine. I crowd closer, sharing my body heat, and stare toward the ocean.

"Okay stop that," Felix says.

"Stop what?"

"That."

I shake my head, chuckling. "What?"

"The way you're breathing."

"I'm not allowed to breathe?"

"Not like that, not all hitched-sounding. Not with the ensuing smack of your lips."

I laugh. "Why not?"

"Because it means you're saying something serious." I hum

non-committedly, and he turns his head toward me. "Won't you?"

He drinks me in, and my veins bloom with warmth.

Waves crash against the shore, and our hearts beat louder.

"Yeah, Felix. I want to say something serious."

"See? I thought so." He points toward the shoreline. "Another walk along the beach?"

I take his outstretched hand. "Haven't we danced around this long enough?"

His eyelids shutter. "This?"

"Us."

Chapter Twenty-Six

FELIX

MORT TWISTS IN FRONT OF ME, FEET FLANKING MINE, HANDS resting against the car roof behind my head. Our chests tap as he leans in. I tip my face to his.

He's right here. Everything I've ever wanted. Right here, admitting he wants me too.

I'm not surprised we got to this—given his comment about hard-ons and the present tense—but I am still amazed.

Amazed, flustered, and uncertain.

"Felix?"

His steady breath mixes with my shaky one. I peer into his eyes and my lips bump his. "I'm afraid you'll break my heart."

"My crush on Roch is long in the past."

"It's there every time I close my eyes. I see you rutting against him, your jaw locked as you come over his stomach."

He pulls back. A salty breeze gusts between us, and immediately I miss him. "What are you talking about?"

"That party you and Roch threw. About a month before he asked Lauren out the first time. You were drunk and sloppily confessing to Roch—to the whole party—you'd be virgins forever?"

"You know about that night?" Mort pales. "It was Roch's—"

"I don't know who suggested it, but you were really into it."

"You . . . watched us?"

Yes. "Not intentionally. It wasn't my drunken ass that pulled you into my room."

"Fuck, Felix."

"I wanted to throw you out, scream at you, but I couldn't. I just froze . . . and then left."

Mort shuts his eyes and sinks back a few steps. He opens the boot and tosses his cap inside. "I'm sorry. I wish you'd never seen that. I wish it'd never happened."

I wish I'd never brought it up.

This evening, dancing with Mort at the base of the lighthouse, had been perfect. Tender, comforting, real. If I'd kept this to myself, I could have given in to the burning desire to kiss him, touch him, *be touched by him.* I'd finally know what that felt like.

Instead, we suffer through weighted silence as we climb into the back of The Groove.

Mort lies on his back—shoes off, shorts and T-shirt on, hand tucked under his head.

I mirror him. Only a foot separates us, but it feels like so much more. Rotating beams from the lighthouse turn the inside of the car gold.

"Comfortable?" he asks quietly once the shadows descend.

I latch onto the opening to push through this weird, aching, sad frustration. "It's surprisingly roomy. Maybe I don't need my own place. Maybe I'll live in the car."

"Your three kids would love that."

I shouldn't ask. I shouldn't . . . "Do you want kids?"

He lets out a tired breath, and I turn my head. Mort's eyes are closed and his jaw is working through some emotion.

Crap. "That was really awkward timing, huh?"

"That depends." He opens his eyes and finds mine. "Are you asking if I want kids with you?"

Yes. No. Maybe? *Crap.*

"Because then the answer is a resounding yes."

Everything around me thickens into a dreamy haze. Mort's calm expression soaks mine in. My mind swims through an incredible pulsing—what is this? *Joy. Bliss. Heaven.*

I want to bathe in it forever, because the shoreline is all fear and insecurities.

I roll against his side and look at him peering nervously up at me.

Panic flares at the implications. I'm toeing the edge of a great cliff; if I fall, I might shatter.

I settle a hand on his chest and feel his thumping heart. It's crazy fast. Like mine.

I cup him just under his ear. "I hate that you loved him, Mort. It hurts. And . . ."

"And?" his voice cracks.

"And no matter how much I tell myself to stop my feelings for you, I can't."

Mort's flickering eyes hold mine with an intensity that sweeps deep in my belly. "Don't."

His fingers curve through my hair to hold the base of my head. Our noses bump. "Please?"

My heart pounds. "I . . . I . . ."

He presses his mouth against mine and holds there.

The throb of this suspended kiss makes me boneless. I sigh and he moves, slotting and re-slotting our lips together. So unexpectedly soft. Tender.

I whimper into his mouth, and he whimpers back, "Please?"

I pull back and look at his hopeful eyes.

The kiss bolts out of me. It's messy and frantic on his hot, buttery mouth.

Mort wraps an arm around my waist and hauls me closer. I plaster myself against the full length of his body: chest to chest, hip to hip, legs settling between his.

He deepens our kisses and steadies my over eagerness, pacing me like he wants this to be a marathon, not a sprint. I want both.

He sucks in my top lip and slides his tongue on the underside, riddling me with an erotic hit of electricity.

I feel his kisses everywhere: the soles of my feet, my ankles, my inner thighs.

Physical sensation steals my thoughts, from the figure-eight looping butterflies to my sinewy limbs against his muscled ones.

He arches into me. I bury my face into his soft neck, sucking in his spicy scent.

He's just as hard as I am. *He's just as hard as I am!*

It's so good, it's too much, it's not enough.

He squeezes my waist in pulses, and I rock against him. I lose all composure, moaning into his mouth as I grip his hair and thrust. My tongue invades his mouth and he sucks on it.

I've never tasted such a kiss before, never felt this overwhelming need for more.

I feel like I'm combusting.

I'm dying.

I'm happy to.

I frantically chase a hand between us, pulling at the buttons of my shorts.

"Felix," Mort says on a pant. "I want to take this step by step with you."

His words break me from the escalating high. I scramble off him until I'm on my knees between his parted thighs, head bowed. "You don't want . . . Because I . . . Sorry. I have no idea what I'm doing." Heat lances through me. I dive to the far side of the car.

"Hey." Mort rolls me back to the middle.

I can't look at him.

"Look at me."

"I want to touch you, Felix. I want to taste you. I also want you to look at me in the morning."

I throw the crook of my arm over my eyes and laugh. "I dare you to make me *stop* looking at you!"

He crawls over me. "Let me see those beautiful eyes."

He nudges my arm away and pins my hands against my head.

An adoring smile glows in the gentle curve of his lips and his crinkling eyes. It's so touching, I almost can't trust that it's real.

I free one of my hands and trace it. "Must be an apparition. Your smiles with me are never this intimate."

He dips his mouth until I feel the outline of his smile against the shell of my ear. "They will be from now on."

He sinks his lower weight against me, and I gasp in pleasure.

Light washes into the car, haloing him.

"How long have you wanted this?" I ask, restraining myself from arching into him.

"It's grown over the years."

"Years?"

"The year before I . . ."

"Left?"

He winces. "I realized I craved being closer to you. And I worried what that meant."

I feather my fingers over his brow. His face is all gentle frankness.

His nose grazes mine and his breath shivers over my lips. His kisses are playful nips and I tip my chin into them, amazed and shocked and scared that this is happening.

I slide my hand over his shoulder like we're about to dance, and I steer him closer.

For once I'm not clumsy. Moving comes easily, effortlessly, instinctively.

I dance my fingers up his neck and kiss him. Mort's return kisses are languid and gentle, like he's savoring every second.

"I'll look at you in the morning, Mort," I whisper. "I will."

"Okay, Felix," he says between shivery kisses down my throat, "I hear you."

He kisses me over my shirt, hovering where he guesses my scar might be—and is. He looks up at me, his eyes clearly saying he wants me to show him.

I swallow.

He comes back up. Teeth scrape over my skin and his nose bumps under my ear. He makes his way back across my cheekbone, bridge of my nose, tip. His kiss melts against my lips, and he slowly deepens it until I'm shivering for more.

"The way you look at me, Felix," Mort says in awe. "It's like—"

"I'm addicted to you?"

He laughs. "That too." He drops another kiss. "It's like you really love what you see."

"And what I hear, feel, smell, and taste."

Mort pauses. "You know all the senses. Well done."

"Bastard. It's more than that. It's this feeling—like you *touch* me."

"Also one of the senses."

I smack him over the back of the head, laughing. "*Inside.* Although it seems to be fading fast."

Mort pops open my fly and palms my erection. "Not everything's fading."

I raise my hips eagerly, urging him to remove my shorts. "I'm afraid it won't ever fade again after this."

"I love the blunt way you exclaim that."

Bantering with Mort as he strips my shorts punches emotion behind my swelling lust. We have a connection. "Kiss me."

Mort frees my leg and races his fingers up my calf and the side of my knee. He spreads my leg and kisses my thigh.

Holy—

He doesn't stop there. With teeth and tongue and stubble he whispers his way to my boxer-briefs.

"Fuck-fuck-fuck-fuck-fuck."

"Scared fuck? Or exhilarated fuck?"

"Both. The latter."

He hesitates. I roll my hips. "I'll look at you tomorrow," I promise. "I'll look at you forever—"

My words are swallowed as Mort buries his head between my thighs and nuzzles my balls through the fabric. The heat of his breath leaks through and I'm back on my *fuck-me* mantra, long drawn-out *fuuuuuucks* that sound like debauched groans. I don't care.

I comb my fingers through his hair—thick and silky—and my palms close over the tops of his ears, the curves pressing like kisses on my skin.

Mort's breathing is harsh and gravelly. He's saying things I can't quite understand. He peels back the elastic—was he asking if he can remove my underwear?

"Yes."

He sits up just as light spills into the car. His lips are raw and his shirt has ridden up.

I push into a sitting position and press my hand against his navel. Mort's breath hitches over the T of my nose.

His lips settle warmly on mine, slotting and re-slotting like our first kiss—but this one feels different. Like the precursor to something more.

His stomach undulates under my touch and I explore up his shirt. His nipple is hard and I rub my thumb over it, loving the way he grips my neck and slides his tongue into me.

I play with his soft chest hair.

He cradles my head and his next kiss sweeps me onto my back. His fingers work my briefs down my thighs.

My fingers fly between us, not to help him with my pants but because I need to feel him. The outline of his hard cock bores into my hand, and Mort chokes out a sexy growl. He grinds into my touch and his eagerness feeds my own. I have never felt so aroused.

He swallows my begging pleas and trails kisses between the buttons of my shirt towards my pulsing cock.

He wrestles my boxers from my thighs and shimmies between my legs, palms clasping my hips.

His lips hover close to the straining, moist tip of my cock. He looks up at me pushing on my elbows. This is really about to happen.

I bite my lip on a moan.

Mort's gaze darkens and his grip on my hips deepens. A hot tongue darts over the head of my cock. I tremble, falling back to the foam floor, and Mort sinks his hot, wet mouth over me.

He grips my base and sucks me deeper, his slippery tongue working me with perfect friction.

I buck into the irresistible heat of his throat.

I apologize and try to refrain, but it feels so good. Mort grips my ass, pushing me into him like he wants me too.

Fuck-fuck-fuck, I really am going to combust.

I squirm, limbs uncontrollable as I give in to the sensation.

Mort hungrily takes me down his throat, his groans

vibrating over the head of my cock. And my mind is blank. I'm saying things, lots of things, but I have no idea what they are.

Mort works his mouth faster around my cock while he shoves his shorts down. His knuckles start jerking over the side of my knee, faster and faster.

I raise my head and—

The sight of Mort sucking me while he viciously strokes his cock sends me over the edge.

I whine that I'm about to come, and Mort sinks his mouth down my cock.

I thrust into his tight throat. I am one long *fuuuuuuuck* as my orgasm barrels into me. I shoot, over and over and over, and it's unlike anything I have ever felt.

Mort groans around me, lengthening the waves of pleasure. Splashes of come hit my thigh.

That's it. I've combusted. It was a good life.

I'm vaguely aware of Mort pulling off and demanding a kiss.

He chuckles into my mouth. I keep him hostage there for long, languid minutes until I can function again.

"Mmm," I say, the universal word for satisfaction.

Mort says it back, and my eyelids flutter closed. A little snooze would feel perfect.

Mort fumbles around, and then a soft blanket settles over me. He curls close and whispers in my ear. "Everything I just did to you, I will do again. Not tonight, maybe tomorrow, definitely in the following week."

He nuzzles under my ear. "Do you know what I'm saying?"

"You're addicted to me, too?"

He nips my jaw. "Yeah, pretty much that."

Chapter Twenty-Seven

FELIX

I PROMISED I'D LOOK AT MORT THE NEXT MORNING, AND I DO. A lot. I'm amazed at what happened between us, and I want to feel this intense level of amazement over and over again.

Mort looks at me with the same intimate, secret smile that he bestowed on me last night . . ..

I'm breathing hard just thinking about it. God, Mort was writhing his body against mine last night. My solid, compassionate, geeky jock lusted over me. I turn the radio on to stymie conversation. I need the drive home to process last night. Because. Wow. And more. *And stop right here on the side of the road and let me taste you.*

But also: *Crap*.

"Want to talk about it?"

"I can't hear you over the music and my ridiculously racing mind—but you look hot."

And he does. Sort of disheveled after a night choked by my

sprawling limbs. His T-shirt looks softer after our night together. I bet it smells of us: musky sweat and hazelnut.

Holy crap, look at him. The tight line of his neck, the width of his shoulders, the curves of his bicep tensing as he shifts gears.

I'm feeling buzzed everywhere.

The way his ass molds to the seat, shorts giving way to blond-haired thighs. And his calves.

Double crap, I'm burning for him.

I don't care about anything other than what he tastes like, how long I can make him come, and when can we continue this?

But I should care.

I should.

Mort reads my need to squash the discussion and calmly drives me to work. We park outside and the music cuts off. I hesitate with my hand on the door.

I look at him.

He looks at me.

"What happens next?" I blurt.

He drums on the steering wheel. "We alert the authorities that you have not, in fact, been kidnapped. Simply that I have stolen you away to do wicked things with your beautiful body."

"Mort!" I say with a scandalized flourish.

"What?" His cap is not enough to hide the glee in his eyes. "You don't want to do naughty things with me?"

Yes, and desperately. But. "I have work, and you have a family to chauffeur."

"After I pick you up from work then?"

"Tiffany needs another driving lesson."

"Are you trying to fill the day to avoid time alone with me?"

"Is it working?"

Mort palms my knee. "What's wrong, Felix?"

Nothing, technically. Only . . . "I'm nervous."

"That comment about stealing you away was mostly teasing. We'll take the heart-hitching as slow as you like."

"I'm not nervous about sex." Well, I am a little.

"I didn't say anything about sex."

I hold my breath, because it's the heart-hitching I'm more afraid of. I'm already in love with him and adding the possibility we could be more . . . makes the love bloom. Makes it a real living thing. And real living things get sick and die . . .

Dread turns my stomach cold and stodgy. What if we end up losing our friendship?

I step out of the car, glancing at his soft expression. My pulse is haywire. "We sure about this?"

Because I'm a coward who can't cope with the response, I shut the door and jog into work.

Three steps into the foyer, a block of heat warms my back and words flitter against my ear. "Keep moving to the bathroom, sunshine."

My pulse flutters in my throat. I manage a nonchalant wave to eighty-nine-year-old Mr. Peterson perched in his wheelchair awaiting his nurse, and head to the bathroom.

Mort follows me in and shuts the door with his boot.

"Are you, crazy?" I exclaim.

"About you? Most of the time."

"Why'd you follow me inside?"

"Follow you. Why did I *follow* you?" He crowds me against the tiled wall. "Turnabout is fair play, don't you think?"

Breathing hard, I can't decide whether to focus on his gaze boring into me or his mouth inching toward mine. "Okay, what is happening right now?"

"I want to kiss you."

"Are you always so forward?"

"Much better than backward." His lips press against mine like silk slipping over skin. "I don't want to go backward with you."

Mort grips the curve of my neck, his thumb tapping my throat. He kisses me firmly with a teasing swipe of his tongue.

And it's perfect.

And my hands are on him. I grab his shoulders, pinching his shirt as I tug him deeper into the kiss. The heat of it sears through to my shaky body, and I can't stop drinking him in.

He draws away, leaving me a tingling mess, mercifully propped up by the wall.

"Are we sure about this?" He fans his hand over my shirt, the imprint leaking to my chest. "I am."

"I feel weird."

"In what way?"

I can't suppress an excited, nerve-wrecked shiver. "Vulnerable. Hopeful. Uncertain. Horny."

He smiles. "I feel three out of those four too. Just not uncertain."

"You're not at all?"

"Well, I can't be certain of the outcome—that's what makes me vulnerable—but I am certain I want to be vulnerable with you." His fingers inch to my unadorned collar, sliding over the exposed skin at my throat. He stares into my eyes with disarming shyness. "Will you be vulnerable with me?"

Mort tells me to think about it and leaves me with a smile.

Thinking about it occupies my day. I'm so distracted, I earn a chiding from my boss.

The afternoon drags. Three times I sneak to the bathroom and start messaging Mort that I want to be vulnerable with him, only to delete it. Better in person.

My phone pings.

Roch: Coming for dinner tonight.

I want Roch hanging around and helping out at home. I truly do. Yet my stomach feels weighted. Does he have to come tonight, when I need time with Mort to myself?

How are we supposed to act around Roch? Around Mum, Tiffany, and the twins? How do we act around each other, for that matter? I want public displays of affection, but maybe not before we've told family.

Roch: Was thinking I'd cook?

I set aside my worries and reply.

Felix: As long as it's not spicy.

Roch: You take the fun out of food.

Roch: Will Mort be there?

Yes. I hope so. He'd better be.

Felix: Probably.

Roch: Excellent. See you guys tonight!

After work, I race outside into a salty summer breeze. Mort rocks around the corner on foot. "Hey, Felix."

"Hi." My body flickers to life like candlelight on a first date. Mesmerizing. Romantic. *What does being vulnerable with Mort look like?*

I imagine us back in The Groove—or a bed—his powerful

naked body looming over mine, his firm grip confidently parting my thighs, the tip of his cock brushing against my balls and skating to my entrance—

Holy crap.

I love this navy shirt on him, a little snugger than his usual ones, showing off his tapered torso. "You ready?"

"Yes."

We stare at each other, and my thoughts don't improve in quality. A nice heat races up my neck.

"God I'd love to know what you're thinking right now."

I lurch in the direction Mort came. "Where are you parked?"

He chuckles, knowingly. "Around the corner."

He catches up and follows beside me. We side-eye each other at the same time and he winks. "How was your day?"

"Hard."

His lips tick up. "I wasn't expecting such a sexy answer, but I like it."

I elbow his side, unable to suppress a laugh. "I meant work was hard. How was your day?"

"I spent most of it at the arcade."

"Dance Dance Revolution?"

He resettles his cap "Yeah."

"You're obsessed."

"Kinda."

The Groove comes into view, and Tiffany is sitting in the driver's seat.

Mort slows his step. "Are you ready for another lesson, followed by a dance lesson with Tiffany, follow by a family dinner, followed by me retreating to my place?"

"You added to our schedule?"

"Every minute chaperoned to ease your nervousness."

I catch Mort's hand and turn toward him. "Mort, I—"

Tiffany beeps the horn and waves.

"Yeah, Felix?"

I can't concentrate with Tiffany watching. "Later."

I throw myself into the back seat and jam between the seats to kiss Tiffany on the cheek. "Sorry again for yesterday. How was Arjun's party?"

Mort buckles into the passenger seat and she looks from me to him.

"I have another item to add to the pro side of learning how to drive. Some of the guys got so pissed and I had to practically carry Gillian to her place. Driving would be so much easier."

"You'd want to be the designated driver?" I ask.

"I think so."

"Thrilled to hear that, Tiff."

Tiffany bounces her palm atop the gearstick. "Okay, let's get this lesson started."

We cruise along the quiet streets around the retirement home. Tiffany concentrates on changing gears. There is a roundabout too, which has her reviving her "Oh. My. God." chant.

Mort makes her exit and enter it three times, until she's confident. After an hour, Mort swaps seats with her and drives us home.

"How do you feel after your fifth lesson?" he asks Tiffany.

Her ponytail whips over the headrest. "Exhilarated. I want to do it again and again. Maybe it was worth working through my fears."

Mort eyes me in the rearview mirror and returns his focus to Tiffany. "Even at the risk of car accidents. Getting lost. Being pulled over. The river flooding and being stuck. A tsunami. Breaking down in the middle of nowhere. Breaking down in the middle of traffic. Driving at night. The seatbelt locking when you need to escape. Black ice. Spending all your savings on a car?"

Tiffany and I gawk at him.

And then I gawk at Tiffany as she says, "Yeah. Even at the risk something goes wrong."

~

AN HOUR LATER, MORT AND I ARE SHOELESS IN THE BACK YARD, instrumental music sailing out of the speaker near Tiffany.

Soft grass tickles my anklebones, but it has nothing on the tickle of Mort's whisper in my ear.

"You're adorable when you stumble over my feet."

"It's hardly adorable."

"The same beats every song intro. I especially love how you catch yourself against my chest. Like you're about to rip my shirt off."

Mort laughs.

"Stop laughing."

He does no such thing, catching Tiffany's eye. "Maybe we should practice from the top again?"

"Or I could throttle you," I mutter under my breath.

He pulls me into position. "My idea's less kinky."

A laugh tumbles out of me. "Stop it, Mort."

"You don't like me teasing you?"

"I like it too much, and it's making me worse at dancing. If Tiffany has to reposition me, I'll die of *mort*ification, and then you'll never hear my answer to your question this morning."

He pumps my hand, laughter simmering to something quieter and more anticipative. Hazel eyes soften and pull me in—

"Well would you look at that?"

Roch's voice rips me out of Mort's arms.

How are we meant to act? My stomach knots with unease.

Mort folds his arms. Is he equally unsure?

The knots tighten.

Does seeing Roch make him realize his feelings for me were

misguided? Is he regretting every whispered word he spoke to me last night? Maybe—

"Felix?"

"Huh?"

Roch frowns.

"We're practicing," I blurt. "For your wedding."

Mort slowly inclines his head.

"Let me show you how it's done." Roch sweeps in and clasps Mort into position like he's done a thousand times before. Despite the height difference, Roch sweeps Mort around the back yard with confidence, poise, and possibly a little possessiveness.

Tiffany sidles up to me. "He's moving in on your man."

"I have eyes." My gaze whips to Tiffany. "Wait, what do you mean?"

"Took me way too long, dammit, but I finally figured it out."

My pulse jumps in my throat.

She bites down on a grin. "Now I understand why you are the way you are around Mort."

"The way I am around Mort?"

"Like he cut out your heart and holds it ransom, and you want it back."

I sink my hand through my hair. "No, Tiff, that's not right."

"It's not?"

I drop my hand and face her. My voice rumbles. "I don't want mine back. I want his."

She hugs me tightly. "I like your version of this story better."

"Keep it to yourself?"

"Mum's the word."

"Not the expression I would have gone for."

"She's doing better—by me, at least. I like that she's trying."

"I'm glad, Tiff." *I'm still waiting for her to apologize to Mort.* "Now, let me get back to fretting."

I watch Roch lead Mort toward the bridge. The music stops and so does Roch. Mort looks like he wants to head back to us but pauses at something Roch says. Their earnest postures are angled toward each other.

Roch pauses his conversation and calls out to me. "Can you please start peeling potatoes?"

It's an obvious ploy to buy them privacy. I prickle from head to foot.

Reluctantly, I disappear inside. Tiffany chats with me, but I can't concentrate. I can't even *find* the bloody potatoes, let alone peel them.

I stare out the window at their figures, twitching every time Mort smiles.

Mum strolls into the kitchen, humming. She pecks Tiffany's cheek and hesitates next to me. She drums painted nails on the counter. "Either of you seen April and May?"

"They're in the bush," Tiffany says. "The glowworm cave."

I lunge toward the door. "Me. I'm on it."

Mum blinks at me curiously, while Tiffany's grin doubles in size.

"Oh shush," I scold, eliciting a laugh.

"Am I missing something?" Mum says.

"Nothing. It's time the twins come inside and wash up. I'll grab them . . ."

Chapter Twenty-Eight

MORT

"WHERE'S LAUREN?"

Roch plucks invisible lint off his shirt. "She's, um, working late."

He's hiding something. But what? His cheeks are flushed and his expression holds an uneasy edge. "Are you two all right?"

"Me and Lauren? Yes! Absolutely, yes." Sounds genuine. "How was your, um, day?"

"You asked me that twice already." Something's distracting him. It's been happening more and more when we're together lately.

"Are *you* all right, Roch?"

He laughs and rolls a hand over his face. "Fuck."

I follow him to the bow of the bridge. Forearms against the rail, he peers at the creek.

Worry simmers in my stomach. "Okay, what's going on?"

"Love the way the sunset turns the water peach."

"Roch."

He curses under his breath and steeples his fingers. "I keep trying to talk to you about this but I keep chickening out."

"You have my full attention." Or at least the parts that aren't scrambling to process the bite from Felix ripping away from me when his brother showed up. Which, to be fair, might hold most of my attention.

"So look, the weekend after New Year's."

I jerk my focus to Roch. "What about it?"

"It will be hot."

"Thanks for the weather forecast."

He flashes me a reproving glance but laughs again. A short, hollow bark. "Lauren has a girl's weekend. Her version of a hen's night, I suppose."

"Okay . . ."

He faces me. "Will you go camping? Just you and me and nature?"

"Is that what you've been so nervous to ask me?"

He ducks his head toward the creek again. "No, it's not. I'll tell you when we're camping. If you're coming. You are coming, aren't you?'

I stiffen. I want to, I do. He's my mate and I'd love to hang out like we used to. But things are burgeoning with Felix and it's a bad time to break the growing intimacy.

I rub my nape. "Tell me what you really want to talk about."

I want to know, but mostly I'm buying more time to navigate my answer about this weekend away with him.

Roch's eyes shift behind me and pause. I follow his gaze to Felix striding across the yard to the bridge. The sinking sun haloes him from hair to hips.

He passes me with a jolt of electricity. All I want to do is sling an arm around him and nuzzle kisses against his neck. Roch be damned.

Roch twists from the edge of the bridge and pinches Felix playfully. "What's up, little bro?"

Felix gives an irritated sigh and glances apprehensively my way. "I'm not little. I'm saving the glowworms from April and May."

"Wouldn't it be quicker via the street?"

Felix's eyes lash toward me, and I know he traveled this way to pass us. I smile softly, and Felix gulps. "I like this way better."

He scurries across the bridge.

I watch until the trees swallow his lithe form.

God, if only I could climb into that head of his. Later, hopefully.

"Where were we?" Roch murmurs.

"You were asking me away for the weekend and telling me your innermost secrets." It's a joke, but Roch pales.

Shit.

I touch his arm in a friendly, supportive gesture.

He buckles, eyes blinking rapidly. "I love Lauren. I truly do. She's my happily ever after."

I frown. "So what's happening? I'm confused."

"So was I. Growing up." He raises his head. "I was confused, Mort."

My spine stiffens. I know where this conversation is heading, and I don't want to go there. A decade ago, yes. Not now.

"Roch—"

"Just listen. I know I kept telling you we were messing around. That I wasn't conforming to toxic straight-guy bullshit, but it was an excuse." I feel for him, but I also feel extremely uncomfortable at the shitty timing of his confession. I've well and truly moved on from Roch—romantically. It almost seems laughable I ever did, when the feelings I have for his brother outshine my feelings for Roch a thousand-fold.

I tense, awaiting the words he struggles to utter. Maybe I can stop him?

"Really, Roch—"

"I'm bisexual. I should have told you earlier. I screwed with your feelings and I'm sorry for hurting you. I wanted to do everything we did, too. I was just too afraid to admit it."

A strangled whimper sounds from the bushes and dread fills my stomach. I know it's Felix, and I know he'll retreat from everything we've started now.

Crumpled in his admission, Roch doesn't seem to have heard his brother.

I scrub a hard hand over my jaw. I want to reassure him I'm fine and be present to talk through his feelings, but *Felix.*

God, Felix.

"I gotta—" I stride toward the bush.

"Oh, sure. Right," Roch murmurs. "Take all the time you need." And more faintly, "I'm sorry."

I race into the bushes just as Felix blinks around a bend. I've left a mess with Roch, and I pray to God I can fix the one with Felix. Stray leaves slap my arms as I pound up the steep incline. The ground levels out and dips. Two more corners, and Felix's bright green Chucks come into view. He's slouched against a moss-covered tree stump before a rocky stream, head tilted back toward the leaves and the speckled bursts of sunset filtering through them.

I slow my pace, removing my cap.

I'm fit, but my breathing is raw and ragged.

I want Felix in my life. More than a friend, more than family.

This situation with Roch is messing things up between us. It was already a sensitive issue, but now . . . Jesus. I can only imagine the insecurities flooding him.

I understand how it appears from his perspective. He will probably always wonder—if Roch had spoken earlier, would I be with him?

Buried in regret, I feel frustrated and stuck. How can I prove he's my number one?

I approach him and Felix slides off the stump, scoops up a handful of pebbles, and starts tossing them, one by one, downstream.

I steel myself at his side.

I'm not giving up on me and Felix. Not for this roadblock. Not for any.

Chapter Twenty-Nine

FELIX

Mort's presence is solid and loud next to me. His aura demands I look at him. I want to, but I don't want him to see how utterly wrecked I am from my brother's heartbreaking confession.

He clears his throat. "Why are you violently skimming stones downstream?"

"I'm not."

"You're refusing to look at me."

I whip another stone into the gentle current. My instinct is to toss out a joke, but the air dancing around my unbuttoned collar reminds me to be honest. "Maybe I'm not the one you truly want doing that."

Who knew my honesty could be so bitchy? Crap.

He clasps my shoulder and steers me toward his solemn expression. "Talk to me."

"It's just . . . a weekend away? He barely has time to help

around the house yet he has time to whisk you away from me for a weekend? Yeah, color me passive-aggressively enraged."

Mort folds his arms over a puffed chest. "You really want to claim this is about Roch helping out more at home?"

I grit my teeth and stare at the bubbling water.

Mort steps closer to me and cups my face. "You're reading too much into this."

I pull out of his hold. "He said he's bisexual! That he *wanted* to do all the things you did together. It's not even necessary to read into it."

"Roch is my friend, Felix. But he's not the one I dream is my boyfriend."

My heart flutters while everything else sinks—I yearn to believe him, but *what ifs* spiral my thoughts to painful places.

"God, I wish you'd believe me."

"I do." I pause. "I want to." I let out a frustrated sigh. "You asked if I'd be vulnerable with you."

He sucks in an audible breath. I study the slight crease in his brow, the blazing eyes, the cap he bends in his hands. "And?"

"I was going to say yes."

Emotion shutters over his face. "And now?"

"I don't know."

"You don't know." His voice breaks, releasing the butterflies in my chest.

"It's just . . . it feels like I'm the only one who has to be vulnerable."

Mort studies me a long time, then he settles his cap on my head and draws me toward him. His words sound swollen. "Ask yourself what I'd be left with if you leave me."

I swallow.

"Ask yourself where I go every day when I leave your house."

Oh. *Oh.* Crap.

"Now ask yourself again if you're the only one who is vulnerable."

"Mort—"

He lets go of the cap and walks backward. "I hope we work through this, Felix. I don't want to miss out on the extraordinariness that is us."

"Why are you walking away?" I call after him, but I don't follow.

"Because I'm sad. Because I need to collect myself. Because you might too."

Right, once again. "I'm sorry. I'm an egotistical bastard."

He grins, but it's pained. "Get the girls inside, eat dinner. We'll talk later, okay?"

"Later?" I flinch at his word choice and he stills. We're both thinking about the infamous "later" he sent me before disappearing for a year.

He approaches me, hazel eyes calm and reassuring. He cups my face and kisses me softly. "I'll be at home. I'll answer every text. I'm never leaving you, Felix. Not unless you want me to."

Mort retreats through the foliage, and I swat my eyes against this swelling tenderness.

Chapter Thirty

MORT

An empty house greets me. Pathetically, I eat canned beans while staring vacantly at my phone. Is it too soon to text Felix? How should I react to Roch?

He's probably eating dinner with the family, so I watch Netflix stand-up comedy, but not even the savviest comedian cracks me. I give up, shower, and lie down with a book. My thoughts drift to the Rochesters until I grab my phone and message Roch.

He doesn't message back, but I keep sending blocks of text until I'm done explaining. I know I should say this to him in person, but the distance makes it easier for both of us. I can tell he's reading, even though he doesn't respond.

I tell him I'm thankful he apologized for screwing with my feelings. I'm truly sorry for the confusion he experienced growing up and saddened he couldn't talk to me about it, but I understand it's not always that simple.

I tell him his friendship means so much to me and I want us to thrive.

I tell him I'm here for him as a friend.

I use the "friend" once more to make a point.

I switch to my chats with Felix. I flop backward onto my pillow, and the bed droops. I need to buy a new bed.

In fact, I should sell the whole place. But I can't. The memories here are mostly of an indifferent dad who didn't look twice at me. But this house is around the corner from the Rochesters', and I love being close.

I suppose I could fix it up. Strip the old wallpaper, paint, remodel, redesign.

Get a new bloody bed.

Dots start jumping on my screen. Felix is typing.

I imagine his gently-corded limbs wrapped around the bedsheets like they embraced me in The Groove. His hair loosely framing his face, pillow pressed against his cheek. Those blue eyes trained on his phone as his fingers swipe the keys.

No message comes through. The dots jump and stop and jump again. And then:

Felix: Night, Mort.

I rub my forehead with my phone and type back.

Me: Night, Felix.

Neither of us preface it with "good."

Chapter Thirty-One

FELIX

I KNOCK ON TIFFANY'S DOOR AND ENTER AT HER "WHAA?"

She's in bed with the covers over her head. I jump on the side of the mattress and pat her legs. "How do you feel about getting up and heading into the city?"

"Not great."

"Why not? We could take a stroll around Oriental Parade and eat ice cream."

Tiffany peels the blankets from her face, revealing a nest of morning hair and a glorious glare. "Have you looked at the time?"

"Sure. We'll be there bright and early. We'll have the beach to ourselves."

"Seven a.m. on New Year's Eve is not bright and early, it's insane."

"Where's your sense of adventure?"

"While I'm thrilled you've finally found yours, crack of dawn beach-tromps are not my idea of a fun adventure."

I search her wardrobe. "Do you want gear for swimming?"

"Not happening, Felix. Whatever energy you so desperately need to burn off, find someone else to help."

"But you're the best, Tiff."

"Awww. Still, no."

"Crap."

Tiffany pulls the blankets over her head again. "Try Mort."

Yes, well. That would be nice. But I'm not sure he's ready yet. I quietly mope out the door. *Maybe the twins are keen on a day's worth of distraction.*

They aren't.

They're harder to rouse than Tiffany. Two snoring lumps under soccer-print duvets.

The scent of nutty coffee catches my nose. My belly flips. Has Mort let himself in? Did he sleep as restlessly as I did and wants to forget space and reconnect over coffee?

I throw myself into the kitchen, and—

"Oh, Mum."

"Felix, morning." She grabs a second mug from the cupboard—Mort's favorite mug—and fills it, adding a splash of milk. "Here you go."

"*You* made coffee."

"Exactly like Mort does, with a pinch of cinnamon in the ground beans."

I take the offered cup and take a slow sip, hoping the warm beverage will ease my disappointment.

Mum eyes me from shirt to shoes. "Are you on your way out?"

"Yes. No. I don't know."

"Is Mort joining you?"

I bury my face in another sip. "Not today."

She looks like she wants to ask more questions. I kind of

want her to. Kind of don't. Like. Her genuine interest in me would be welcome, but any commentary . . . not so much.

"Have you tried Roch?"

I blink. "Huh?"

"You tried getting the girls to go out with you to no avail. How about trying your brother?"

It's . . . an awkward suggestion. And yet.

Maybe I need to talk with him before meeting Mort.

I nod to Mum, pull out my phone and check a few details online. When I have some options, I dial Roch's number.

"Jesus, Felix," he says, groggy as hell. "This had better be an emergency."

"You and me. We're spending the day together."

"Lauren and I are coming over this evening."

"And before that, we're getting up to no good."

"I have food to prepare."

"And after we're done cooking, we'll check out suit stores."

"I thought we'd do that after the New Year."

"There's a New Year's Eve sale at Suit West."

Roch hums. "Yep. Okay. If you can make it to my place, I'm all yours."

"You're a bus ride away." I hang up, triumphant for all of two seconds before I'm hit with a wave of nausea. *He and I have to talk . . .*

Mum cradles her mug and looks over it to me. "You're not a bus ride away."

"Hmm?"

"You're a car ride away."

"Mort can't—"

"Not Mort. Me."

I re-grip my mug and lean against the counter. "You'll drive me?"

"Yes."

"You haven't driven in over a year."

"I'm pretty sure it's like riding a bike."

"No, I mean . . . you haven't wanted to."

She looks at me. "I can't let fear ruin my life forever. I want to drive you. If you'll let me."

"Yes." I swallow. "Yes, I'll let you."

~

I JUMP INTO MUM'S HONDA, AND AFTER A GEAR-GRATING start, we peel away from the curb.

We're quiet—contemplative and cautious about what this means. We reach for the radio at the same time, and quietly chuckle. She pulls back and I turn it on.

"Here Comes The Sun" swells around us.

I see her and Mort singing in the kitchen after school.

It feels like the dream is so close, and still impossibly unreachable.

~

I MEET ROCH. I HELP HIM COOK FOR OUR NEW YEAR'S EVE celebration. I don't say anything about Mort.

My cheeks burn the entire morning though, and I know I have to broach the subject eventually. Somehow.

We take his car into central Wellington to Suit West and step inside a busy store, filled with soon-to-be grooms and the occasional woman shaking her head at ill-suited males.

I mean, I know there's a sale, but I didn't expect the place to be this full. "What are all these guys doing buying suits today?"

"Maybe they all have little brothers who drag them here."

"And I thought I was special."

"You are special, Felix. Very, very special."

I scowl at him.

Gentle music laps at our ears and an employee asks if we'd like any help. Roch and I wave him away with a casual 'just looking.'

I lead Roch to the corner of the store where shirts line one wall, and cravats and ties occupy the other. I scan a large glass drawer displaying fancy bow ties.

I tap over a sleek silver number. "That's nice."

Roch doesn't look. He leans his hip against the drawer and crosses his arms. "You drag me out of bed early and insist on a day together." His voice sounds dry, like he might suspect what's going on. "What's up?"

"I miss you?" I try lamely.

He casts me a reproaching look. "And?"

"Okay." I stare at the bow ties until they blur. "This is about Mort . . ."

"Oh." Roch shifts. "Last night?"

"Yes."

His voice wobbles. "I fucked up, Felix."

"Huh?"

"I'm the reason Mort didn't stay for dinner last night."

He thinks I'm wondering what happened between them. He thinks I don't know. That he's the reason Mort left. *It's not your fault.*

I squeeze away the image of Mort's hurt face beholding me by the creek.

"Why do you think that?" I force out. I want to know. I need to know the exact extent of his feelings for Mort. But, ugh.

"I said some stuff."

I feign intense interest in a red bow tie. The same color as Mort's cap . . . "What stuff?"

"He came over for pizza last month and we got talking about some of the things we did as kids."

"By 'things' you mean"—I open the drawer and hold up

the pinned bow tie, trying not to crush the velvet it's set on —"making out?"

Roch swallows audibly. "Yeah. He told me upfront that I gave him false hope for years."

"He said that?"

My stomach sinks to somewhere around my knees. This conversation is not giving me the reassurance I crave.

Roch continues, "Hearing that made me feel ashamed."

"Why was that?" My voice comes out choked.

"It slammed into me how much my own insecurities were hurting him." He picks out the silver bow tie I first eyed and a cream one with gold threading. "Which do you like better?"

"The silver." I snag an employee and ask for one of this color to try on. He brings us one and a shirt. He offers to tie it for us, but we decline the help and Roch dresses in a changing booth. He comes out in the shirt, collar lifted, and I realize I hold the bow tie. At the large mirror, I slip the length of silver around his neck. "Your own insecurities?"

I can't lift my eyes to his, but I note his deflating shoulders.

"I'm bisexual, Felix."

I try to act surprised, but I'm not sure my "Oh" sells it.

I glimpse Roch's frown in the mirror.

Not wishing to confess to eavesdropping, I hurriedly move the conversation along. "Bisexual. That's . . . well . . . but you're happy with Lauren, right?" I overheard him say he loved her, but I need to see it in his eyes as he says it again. "I mean, just because you're bisexual doesn't mean you love her half as much." I sound vehement, and Roch mistakes it for activism.

"I should have come out to you years ago."

I try to stop myself, but I can't. "And Lauren?"

"She knows. Actually, she's known since high school. She was the only one I felt I could talk to about it."

"Communication is key to a successful loving relationship. You two clearly are meant for each other."

Say you love her. "Felix?"

"Yes?"

"I don't want to force a change of subject on you if you're not ready, but . . . I want you to know if you ever wanted to talk to anyone—I'm here for you."

My head jerks up and I catch the *'it's okay if you are . . . you know, too'* look shimmering encouragingly in his eyes.

"Oh man. Is it so obvious I'm gay?"

Roch doesn't even raise a brow in fake surprise. "I might have noticed you noticing Mort."

"When?"

He frowns again, like the answer should be obvious. "Growing up."

"Yes, well. Apparently subtlety is an art I don't possess."

"Others figured it out too?"

"Everyone, I'm sure."

"Even Mort?"

Especially Mort. "Um, yes. He knows."

Roch nods. "I told him I'm bisexual too. That's why he didn't come to dinner. I think I made him uncomfortable. He made sure to emphasize our friendship when he wrote back last night."

I want to dive into his pocket, steal his phone and read those messages.

I mess up the knot and have to start over.

Roch eyes me in the mirror. It makes me fumble with his tie more until I can't take the soft look he's giving me.

"What?"

"I just hope you find a good man to make a family with."

I have.

"Maybe Mort can introduce you to some of his friends."

"Because it could never work with Mort?"

It's a punch to the gut when he laughs. "Probably a little awkward. Seeing as . . . well . . ."

"Your past?" I finish for him. I don't want to ask, even if I need to know. I pull the longer side of the tie over and under the other, pinching the material hard. "Did you love him? *Do* you love him?"

"I did love him. I do love him."

I'm going to throw up.

Roch weasels a finger under the bow tie. "A little too tight, there. A lot too tight."

"You love him?" I repeat. I want to know, I need to know, but I can't bear to hear those three little words from my brother's lips.

He sighs. "That's why it hurt so much when he left."

My eyes are locked on his, but I'm not seeing him. I'm seeing Mort slipping out of reach. Can I be with Mort if my brother harbors romantic feelings for him—even on a small level? Would it ruin my relationship with him? Would it eventually fracture the family?

Would loving Mort be wrong? It should be, right? So why is my mind trying to find ways it might work?

I look away, throat tight.

The truth is bubbling to the surface and it's messy.

"I love him," Roch says simply, and my belly and head scramble to process his declaration.

I'm waiting for a "but . . ." from him. For an "I'm not *in* love with him." But Roch doesn't give me that.

He murmurs, "I mean, we've had our ups and downs, but he's my best friend."

Chapter Thirty-Two

FELIX

I almost go straight to bed when Roch and Lauren drive us home. Just to sleep off the turbulence in my belly.

Instead, Tiffany plants a flute of chilled bubbly in my hand and propels me toward the disco-ball-lit lounge, where the family is singing karaoke into scratchy microphones.

Throughout warbling love songs, and a half-dozen Pax Polo and Tepid Creek hits, I keep glancing at the door. Like maybe if I watch the speckled light shift over the wood hard enough, I might beam Mort here.

"Where is he?" Everyone is asking where he is. April and May with determined—and disappointed—scowls, Tiffany with calmer introspection—gaze darting from Roch to me, and even Mum with a soft frown and what might be detectable concern. Every time they ask, my stomach turns dinner to slush, and Roch looks guiltily to his sympathetic fiancé. Even though it's not his fault.

I pretend everything's fine, failing at my vow to Mort not to fake it anymore. Every smile empties me until finally I can't handle it anymore, can't force back the sting in my eyes. I steal into my room, strip, and slip into worn pajama bottoms and a singlet that chokes my torso tightly.

It's close to midnight, but I don't care a jot. I want to crawl under my covers and sob out a litany of frustrated curses. I want to . . . I don't know. Go back to yesterday, dancing with Mort in the back yard, my belly hopping with excitement for his next touch.

Roch and Lauren's laughter curls up through the house and it—infinitesimally—eases me to hear it. Their love is there. It shows. It has showed all evening. And there are no secrets between them. Roch doesn't hide any of his feelings about Mort from Lauren. They spent most of our car ride here talking about how Roch messed up apologizing to Mort about leading him on as a teenager. About wishing he'd told Mort he was bisexual years ago. That frankness . . . it's a good thing, isn't it? It puts a different slant on Roch's confession of love for Mort.

His "he's my best friend" could mean he loves Mort platonically, not romantically.

And if it is more than that?

I pick up Mort's cap off my dresser and bring it to my nose. I inhale his dry grass and lemony scent and my stomach cinches.

The terrifying thing is, whatever Roch feels for Mort—

Tiffany barges into my room with two flutes of sparkling wine and a knowing look. "Tell me what's wrong."

I don't deny it, just slump onto the end of the bed, curling Mort's cap. "He's not here."

"So ask him over. He has two minutes before the countdown. He can hotfoot it."

"I'm not sure he wants to."

"Have you texted him?"

I have. "He said he's drinking a quiet beer in the garden."

"There's beer and a garden here."

And his family. April and May singing Beatles songs with Mum. Roch dancing the cha-cha and foxtrot with Lauren. Tiffany in a tremendously insightful mood.

"Okay, spill," she demands, lounging against the doorframe, hair spilling over her shoulders, down for once. "What did you fight about?"

"Who said we fought?"

"Felix, Mort finds *any* excuse to be here. Besides, your early morning wake-up call is starting to make a lot of sense . . ."

I wedge on the cap and lower the rim over my blurring eyes. I could tell her about Roch loving Mort, and it would be part of the reason I'm miserable. But. It's not just that. It's barely that. "He was all reasonable and mature and willing to risk everything and I had a fit of selfish insecurity."

"Okaaaay."

I flop back on my bed, cap popping off my head. "I didn't see past myself and I . . . I hurt him."

"I'm sure he'll forgive you. Just apologize."

I groan and sit upright. "I need that wine."

She holds the flutes away, even though she's across the room. "Hang on. You don't think he'll forgive you?"

"That's the thing, Tiff. I'm fairly sure he already has."

"Where's the problem, then?"

I stab my chest with a finger. "I need to do more. I need to trust, you know?"

"Acknowledging that is a start. What else?"

"Forget studying law. You should study psychology. Become a shrink."

"What else, Felix?"

"I need to support him with *his* vulnerabilities."

This is what has been gnawing at me deeper than Roch's

confession. The whole day, all of last night, I recall Mort's choked voice telling me he's sad.

And then I hear the words he uttered before that, the only words I should have needed. *Roch's not the one I dream is my boyfriend.*

"Vulnerabilities?" Tiffany asks, jerking my thoughts to Mort alone in that damn house.

I close my eyes, pain and sympathy and anger lancing through me at the image. I hate his dad for never showing him love. I'm angry at Mum for ever taking hers away. Mort needs better. He needs to sell that stupid house. He needs to surround himself with good memories and associations. He needs his family. Us. Me.

He needs me.

And where am I? At the end of my bed stewing through feelings while he's undoubtedly doing the same thing. Alone. No Tiffany, no Roch, no one for support.

I bolt to my feet.

"Vulnerabilities?" Tiff queries again.

My voice cracks with urgency. "I've got to go."

I grab Mort's cap and shove my feet into my jandals.

Tiffany leaps aside and I storm downstairs, past the rest of my family counting down from ten, and blast out the door.

Cheers and hoots and stray fireworks shoot into the dark night. Wind pushes warmly at my back, urging me faster.

My jandals slap over concrete and I skid through the gravel of a neighbor's driveway.

I punch at my phone, texting Mort to meet me at the front of his yard. I want to simply rock up at his door, but I know how sensitive he is about his home, despite him never mentioning it. *No Rochester has ever been inside.*

Mort is coming out of his house when I enter his gate. He's in low-slung jeans and an opened shirt revealing a white tank top, and bare feet. He's gloriously handsome—even with the apprehensive expression he wears as he closes the distance between us.

"Fel—"

"Happy New Year," I blurt, anxiously hugging my arms. "You didn't come over tonight. I hoped you might."

"Fel—"

"April and May were mad at you," I toss out jokingly. "I had to stop them devising a plan to fill your letter box with elephant toothpaste."

"Felix?"

I finally look at his face, his expression softened. A hint of a hopeful smile at his lips.

"Why are you here?" he asks.

My belly rises and falls, and inside I'm yelling: because it doesn't matter if Roch loves you! I want you. I want the extraordinariness that is *us*.

And more: because I want to be with you while we fight our insecurities.

And ultimately: *because I love you. Fuck, I love you.*

My mouth feels dry and my tongue sticks to the roof of my mouth; my words come out like sandpaper over metal. "It's officially New Year's Day—I assumed you'd still be up celebrating."

That's what comes out? Celebrating?

"Celebrating?" He raises a disbelieving brow.

I mentally punch myself. "I suppose not."

Mort's gaze tracks over me from cap to jandal, and his lips quirk. "You're here in your pajamas."

"I wanted to"—crawl under my covers and cry—"go to bed."

His brow arches astutely. "You didn't want to . . . celebrate?"

I drop my gaze to his large, bare feet.

His voice rumbles softly. "It's just past midnight."

"Yes."

"Why'd you come here?"

"I really wanted to wish you a happy New Year." I might as well slip on some gloves and start boxing my face. Why is this so nerve-wrecking?

"Happy New Year."

I slouch against the crumbling brick fence and Mort mirrors me, the letterbox jammed between us. I fidget with the old-school flag atop it.

Mort studies me and my face heats.

He presses his fingers onto the curved letterbox, near mine but not touching. "Are you here to talk about us?"

I shake my head. "No."

"Because I'm hoping you are."

I lift my chin, looking at his sleep-wrecked hair and stubble-covered jaw and the caution deepening his eyes. "No," I say again. "I'm not here to talk about us, Mort. I'm here to talk about you."

Surprise jerks his posture. "Me?"

I tremble as I hold on to his gaze. My heart pounds like it's trying to run away from me. "Yes, because you're not just my boyfriend, you're my friend, and—"

Mort sucks in a breath. "Say that again."

"You're my friend—"

He tries to give me a reproachful look but his lips are tugging at both sides. "The other part."

"I don't know," I muse. "Will you call someone to witness the moment?"

He laughs. "No, this moment is just for me."

That's what I want it to be. Just for him. I inch my fingers to his until were touching. Until currents pass between us, amplifying my jittery stomach. "You're my boyfriend."

"I'm your boyfriend," he casts his face toward the charcoal sky. He closes his eyes and his smile is one hundred percent elation. He absorbs the moment and turns to me. His gaze strokes my face, lingering on my mouth.

I bite my lip. "You're making it hard for me not to kiss you right now."

Mort leans over the letterbox. "Good."

I laugh. "Not yet. I came here for you. I'll get to the point in a moment." I hold up my shaking hand. "When I'm not swamped with all these fluttering butterflies."

"Fluttering butterflies?" He smirks.

"What? I'm no longer afraid of a few romantic words, Mort."

His laughter embraces me.

Encouraged, I continue, "But I have been afraid of being with you. Of never knowing if you'd be wishing I was Roch instead."

"I—"

"No, this isn't about that. I'm segueing into what I'm trying to say."

Mort waits patiently while I flounder about.

I roll my shoulders and channel the energy pulsing from him into me. "I'm not the only one who has fears. I see you as a man who is all together and strong and confident—and you are all those things, but that doesn't mean you don't have vulnerabilities."

I stare at his house, a rundown villa with breaking exterior paneling and heartbreaking childhood memories. "I always thought your biggest scar was Roch not loving you back. But it's not." I gesture to the villa. "This is not 'just a house.' This is your biological family never loving you."

Pain shivers in Mort's eyes. "Yeah."

"The only real family you've had is us."

He nods.

"If we don't work out, you risk losing your family." I don't mean I would ever suggest my siblings not talk to Mort, but they might withdraw from him nonetheless.

His eyes glisten and he blinks hard.

I slide my fingers over the back of his hand and thread them through his until I feel the cool bite of the letterbox on my fingertips. "Yet you're willing to try this with me."

"Absolutely." His voice is unwaveringly strong, decided, and it blasts me with warmth.

"Mort? How does living here make you feel?"

He pinches his gaze at the villa for so long, I think he might not answer. Then he pulls his hand out from under mine, scrubs his face, and laughs hollowly. "Empty. Sad. Lonely."

Hearing him admit it squeezes my chest. "I couldn't stand the thought of you here alone tonight. I came here with this urgent need to protect you. To tell you to sell the house and sell immediately. But I . . ."

"What?"

"I don't know if you should."

His voice lowers curiously. "Why not?"

I look at him. "We'll never be truly happy if we run away from facing our fears."

"What are you saying?"

"When shit dads give you shit houses, maybe you have to reclaim them for yourself."

Mort murmurs, "Even if some days it's painful simply walking up to the front door?"

I push off the fence and swat the brick crumbs from my pajama bottoms. "I will help you." I hold out a hand for him. "Shall we?"

He slides off the fence and takes my hand. I walk two steps up the path before his resistance tugs me back.

He stares at his house over my shoulder. "I've been wondering what to do with this place."

"I'll support whatever decision you make. If you decide to reclaim, we'll make positive memories in there."

Mort glances at me and to the façade again. "We?"

I twist and back up into Mort, until his firm chest claps against my back. I pull his arms over my shoulders and heave his weight off the ground.

"What are you doing?"

"Bridal style or flipped over my shoulder might be asking too much, you big lug," I gasp.

I grip his arms and attempt to palm his thigh over my hip.

Mort barks out a laugh and positions himself, legs locking around my waist.

I stagger up the path, cursing, pulled forward by the shock and delight in Mort's chuckles feathering through my hair.

I drag him onto the porch and push open the door. Stepping over the threshold, Mort whispers in my ear. "We're making quite the entrance."

"This moment will be memorable, then."

He slides off me and I face him. His expression flickers with tenderness and my entire body tingles. This is right. "They're all memorable, sunshine."

I look deep into his eyes, softly hazel in the muted light of his hallway. "But this one especially. On the night we committed to being vulnerable together. On the night we became boyfriends."

Mort sucks in a quiet breath and cradles the back of my head. His kiss is soft, delicate, full of meaning.

I take that meaning with a smile, and deepen it. I grab him by the hips as I slide my tongue into his hops-laced mouth. He groans into the kiss, fingers curling my hair, and he kicks the door shut behind him.

"I have another idea how to make better memories here," I murmur over his lips, his jaw, his ear.

His breath hitches. "How?"

I push him back against the door, drop to my knees on the spongy welcome mat, and slide my hands around his hips to the front of his jeans. With a lingering look at his slackened smile and disarmingly weighted gaze, I tug open his top button.

Chapter Thirty-Three

MORT

I SUCK IN A BREATH, SHOULDERS STIFF AGAINST THE DOOR panels, and let it out slowly.

I'm still fighting the swooping sensation in my gut from Felix showing up and hauling me over this threshold.

I'm so damn relieved he came over. So elated. So *touched.* Desire to be close throttles my chest and pulses my cock.

God, Felix is beautiful on his knees before me, cheeks flushed with nervousness, hair escaping the edges of my cap, lips wet from darting his tongue.

"Plenty of ways we can make memories . . ."

He hums while his fumbling fingers pull my jeans and underwear to my thighs. My freed erection stretches toward his parted lips. His ghosting breath over the tip has me shivering, glad I'm propped against the door.

I pinch my cap back to see more of his face.

His sexy gaze flickers to my cock with hunger and . . .

determination. His hand trembles against the scar at my inner thigh. "I've been imagining this since that night in The Groove. Rubbish. Before that. Years. Forever."

On "forever," Felix's hot mouth tentatively closes over the head of my cock.

He moans as he tastes me, then glances for reassurance he's doing this right. I slide a comforting hand through his hair and squeeze gently. "You're perfect."

He sucks me deeper.

"Ah, God." Sensation spreads like wildfire through my legs, arms, scalp, chest. Jesus. Intense desire and tenderness spiral around each other like a caduceus. It's almost too much.

I throw my head back against the door.

Felix tongues my slit. The mouth that captures me with its words is slaying me now.

He works me tentatively. Gentle, like his soul, but each of my littered curses grows his confidence. He gives in to his own pleasure.

His enthusiasm, the way he cups my balls, his darkened lust-fogged eyes, the hand massaging against my hip . . .

All my nerve endings are burning.

Felix's fingers drag over my wiry pubes and curl around the base of my cock. He squeezes me and feeds my length down his throat like he's desperate to be closer, deeper.

I love the slick sounds he makes and the unabashed groans. I love how he lets go despite his nervousness.

His eyes roll up to mine, and the blazing connection between us sends me over the edge. I rock into his mouth and warn him I'm there. He steals more of my affection when he stubbornly sucks me—

"God!" My orgasm rocks through my body. My head falls back as I shoot down his tight throat.

When the waves ebb, Felix pops off me, swallowing. He licks his lips and meets my eye coyly. "Was that . . . okay?"

Ah, Felix.

I haul him up to me and crush him into a kiss. "You're so damn sexy. Your mouth . . . magic."

I feel his erection twitch against my naked thigh. I whisper in his ear, "Living room or kitchen? We have more memories to make."

His answer tickles over my neck. "Living room."

I stomp out of my jeans, herd him to the couch, and press him lengthwise against it. I toss my cap aside and levy my weight onto him.

We make out like teenagers, hot and heavy, and then we slow down, memorizing each other between each press of our lips. My hand wanders up his tight tank top and I stop at his belly button.

My fingers brush over his outie. Felix clasps my hand, stilling me. His eyes meet mine, beholding me with trust that makes my heart thump. His eyelashes kiss skin when he briefly closes his eyes. "Mort?"

"Yeah?" My answer is a croak.

"Up an inch and to your right." He lets go of my hand and my fingers stay at his navel. When he frowns, I find my voice.

"I don't just want to touch it."

"You can look, too."

"I'll want to talk."

Felix sucks in breath and lets it out slowly. He pushes me off him and draws his tank top over his head. It falls to the carpet, and his smooth back rises and falls as he takes a moment. He lies back down, exposed, searching my expression.

Beneath his firm, hairless chest, just under his ribs, sits a glossy white scar. I tentatively reach out to trace the taut line. Felix's stomach undulates under my touch, and his expression shutters as if reliving the memory.

A pained lump fixes in my throat. "I'm sorry."

"It saved Mum's life, so . . ."

"I should have been there."

He's quiet and then, softly, "Yes."

I press my fingers against his scar until I feel a pulse between us. "The worst mistake I've made, leaving then. I—"

Felix touches my face. "I forgive you, Mort."

A strangled whimper escapes me. I hadn't realized how much I craved hearing this.

"Mort?"

A heavy breath floods out of me.

"Are you . . . crying?"

My eyes sting. Yeah, I might be. "I don't expect perfection. I know I'll make mistakes and shitty decisions. I know you will too. That's life."

"You're right."

"But if there is one mistake I could take back, I promise you, Felix, it would be leaving when you donated your kidney. And ignoring the inner voice that begged me to stay."

His hand drops to my bicep and he squeezes. "Mort . . ." He swallows.

"Did it hurt? Were you afraid?"

"Yes, and yes."

"Shit."

"But I also felt good after. I gave life. That's . . . well, some might say that's Godlike." He grins, and a laugh jumps out of me.

"Ah, sunshine." I drag a delicate kiss over the length of his lips.

His gaze snags mine with intense adoration. He grabs my nape and draws me in for another kiss.

His erection bores against my lower belly and I need to give him release.

I eagerly shove down his pajama bottoms, kneel between

his thighs and deep-throat him until he's a jerking mess under me, punching the air with curses as he comes.

"Holy crap you're amazing," he says. I collapse next to him on the couch.

"I know."

He snickers into a lazy kiss that feels light and natural, like something we've been doing all our lives.

"This reclaiming the house idea of yours . . ." I steer Felix's arm around my waist and lock his leg over my knees. "I'm really into it."

Felix slides closer and welds my mouth with kisses. "They won't all be sexual memories, but I'm hoping a lot of them will be. Especially our firsts."

He shivers, and I feel his apprehension simmering under his excitement. I whisper a kiss over his cheek. "There's no rush, sunshine."

"I don't know," he whispers back in my ear. "I've been imagining you inside me since I was sixteen. Pretty sure I've waited long enough."

I groan against his neck and nip him when he squirms. "Another day."

"No more stamina, old man?"

I swat his ass and he wriggles against me. "No more condoms."

"Grab the keys, there's a service station two minutes down the road—"

I roll onto him, laughing. Judging by his pinched eyes and sudden yawn, I know he's joking too.

We smile dizzily at each other.

"Happy New Year, Felix."

"Happy New Year, Mort."

We fall asleep smiling, wrapped around each other, a few family announcements away from everything I could possibly want.

Chapter Thirty-Four

FELIX

"How do you feel," I ask, tugging on a pair of Mort's shorts to avoid the questions that will arise if I slink through my front door in my pajamas, "about breakfast?"

Mort eyes the shorts and frowns.

Guilt rides up my throat. I eye him doing up the last button on his shirt, dampness from his shower leaking through. I should have showered with him instead of fretting about how to tell the family about us.

"If you're thinking about Breakfast at Tiffany's, then I feel very good about it."

I was thinking about heading to a café. A nervous jolt claims my tongue for a few beats while I think about taking him home. But why would anyone blink twice? Mort always finds excuses to stay at our place. Eating breakfast together won't be new.

Reassured, I smirk. "*Breakfast at Tiffany's*, huh. How long have you been holding onto that one?"

He closes the gap between us, spreading a citrusy scent. "A bloody long time."

There are kisses. Lots of them, bumping me toward the front door. We part when we hit the path and I fiddle with my phone to stop myself taking his hand. Taking some kissing. Taking him. Rubbing myself over him on our front yard isn't exactly how I want the family finding out.

How do I want them finding out?

No, that isn't the issue.

How will they react when *they find out?* That's the issue.

Tiffany answers the doorbell with an ultra-knowing grin. "Why do I suspect this will be the best year yet?"

Mort looks quizzically at us, and I'm certain he's decided Tiffany knows about us.

"Breakfast," I say, tromping inside, my gut a whirlpool. I hope the pancakes I smell will calm me.

April, May, and Mum beeline out of the dining room with their plates. Clattering dishes fill the background as Mort slinks behind me.

I itch to lean back and wrap his arms around my waist, but Mum hums in the background and I jerk toward a seat.

Mort snags the one next to me; I pass him a clean plate and we pile on leftover pancakes and drizzle them with maple syrup.

Sweetness explodes over my tongue, but I barely taste it. Mort's curious look is all I see.

After my third pancake—and Mort's thirtieth look—I elbow his side. "What?"

A hot palm lands on my thigh. "Where do we go from here?"

My thigh flexes under his touch. "Well . . . I have a shift today."

"Felix," he chastises softly. I know what he meant and he

knows it. "You're wearing my shorts. You keep looking at the kitchen door every time Dolores makes a sound. Are we waiting to tell your family?"

Yes. No. I mean . . . *what will they think?*

He leans in and whispers, "It's okay if you're afraid. It's okay not to rush this."

"But? I hear a but."

He laughs and rubs my thigh. "Ah, well . . . No, that's it."

I scowl and prod my fork toward him. "I know you, Mort Campbell. There's a but."

His gentle laughter mellows, and my synapses crackle under his deepening gaze. "But," he says, "I really want to kiss you."

That soft frankness cleaves through every anxiety. I set my fork down and twist until my knees bump his outer thigh. I fold forward, heart banging hard.

Mum and Tiffany chat in the kitchen. April yelps somewhere down the hall.

My pulse changes, but not my decision. I slide my hand across his shoulder and nape. "Kiss me."

His lips descend to mine and he tastes like I'm driving down a sudden dip in the road surrounded by fields of dry grass and lemon trees.

He licks the maple syrup from the bow of my lips, and I hum into his kisses. "By the way, you guessed correctly. Tiffany already knows about us. She figured it out."

He hums back, "She's clever, that one." He pauses, lips vibrating against mine. "The twins know too."

I draw back incredulously. "They do? When? How?"

Mort glances over my shoulders. "Just now. They've caught us kissing."

I swivel around and see my twin sisters gaping at us from the doorway. "And we approve," April says. "Now if you're done bumping lips, Mort, can you help with our go-karts?"

Mort finds my hand under the table and weaves my trembling fingers through his.

"I have to drop your brother to work, but when I get back, we'll put the finishing touches on them, okay?"

"Yes!" May pumps her fist. "You go back to . . . whatever, and we'll set everything up." April drags her from the room.

Well. Okay then.

I sink into my chair. "This is real. People know about us."

Mort's arm brushes mine. "What are your thoughts on telling your mum? Roch?"

I gnaw on my lip. "Yes. Um. Maybe not everyone at once?"

I suspect Mum has been wondering if we're together for a while. I don't think she'll be shocked. Whether she'll be pleased is another story.

Roch, though. Roch has no idea.

I worry most about telling him.

"Whenever you're ready, Felix."

"Thanks, love."

"Love?"

Heat burns up my neck. "If you like it?"

Mort leans toward me, feathering a lock of hair out of my eye. "I *love* it."

I can't help it; I snort and fall into another kiss.

"—Ohhh."

I jerk back. Pulling her hair into a bun, Tiffany approaches the table. "Tiffany, hey. Again. What's going on, sis? How's it hanging?"

Both Mort and my sister blink at me.

"Yes, well," I explain, shrinking back into my chair. "This is still new to me."

"No shit." Tiffany smirks and nibbles on a pancake. "So . . . the girls are talking."

"Talking?"

Tiffany bites her pancake. "They blurted out your kissing

escapade to me in the kitchen. Mum heard."

"Mum!"

Tiffany nods. "The only thing she said was that it happened quickly."

I scoff. "No, no it didn't."

Mort chuckles. "I'd say it took . . . forever."

His affectionate look throws me back to last night. To taking him in my mouth as deep as I could have him—and I want deeper still. I want him inside me as he looks at me like I'm the most amazing thing in his life.

"What are you thinking?"

I flush and wave a hand absently toward the kitchen. "This is all very . . . anti-climactic."

Mort rests his cool forehead against my clammy one. "Are you disappointed?"

"No, no. Maybe a little? I was preparing to fight for you if she got upset."

Tiffany pipes up, taking the words that stretch silently between us. "That could still happen, Felix. When you tell Roch."

Telling Roch. The burden follows me over the next couple of days to work, to Mort's house—where I've been sleeping in his godforsaken bed—and to the dance studio, where Tiffany is finishing her first lesson of the year.

Mort and I are sharing salty fries in the arcade, not a drop of hot sauce in sight.

Roch hovers between us anyway. Smack-dab in the forefront when Mort's phone rings.

"It's Roch." Mort glances at me over his phone.

"Right." I swallow. "Take it."

Mort locks his feet around my ankle under the table and

answers.

"Roch, hey . . . No, I'm fine. We're fine. You got my messages, right? . . . Camping?" His eyes seek mine but I busily stuff fries into my mouth. "I'll get back to you tomorrow . . . Yes, I still have gear." He snorts and rolls his eyes. "I'll let you know."

He slides his phone into his pocket, eyeing me. "How are you feeling?"

"Like a jealous prick. You didn't tell him."

"Did you want me to?"

"No!"

He deserves to know, and I want to be open about Mort and me, but . . .

Telling him feels difficult.

I clear my throat and try again. "I mean, together, right? Face to face."

Mort pops a fry into his mouth. "You might want to memorize this nose. Might not look the same after we tell him."

I scoff. "Roch would never hit you. Hit on you, maybe. But never hit you."

Mort thumbs my inner wrist. "Do you worry that will happen if I go camping with him?"

A little. Maybe a lot. "I—"

Tiffany squeezes between us on the bench, beaming. "Lauren just offered me a job for her and Roch's wedding."

Mort and I share a smirk. "And what do you think of it?"

"OMG, LOL, WTH and a few other acronyms." She's practically bouncing. "Want to hit some arcade machines?"

"Cruis'n World?" Mort suggests.

Tiffany flies off the seat. "Buckle up."

They race cars boldly, laughing and screaming at their screens. I admire them while unconsciously slinking to the Dance Dance Revolution machine.

Two teenage boys are jumping their hearts out. When it

finishes, they check their scores and high-five each other. "Fourth and fifth place overall. We're almost there."

"After a thousand bloody dances. How the hell did that guy score so high on all the songs? Must have triple A's everywhere. Fucking God."

I butt in. "Mort practically lives this game. That's why he's number one."

They look puzzled. "Mort? Oh, right. Yeah, he's good too." The taller one nudges his curse-prone friend. "Drink break?"

They scuttle away, and curiosity lures me to the screen. I scroll to the top scorers and freeze. An axis tips inside me, releasing every butterfly that's ever existed.

I return to Mort and Tiffany, dizzy.

"And . . . thank you for teaching me to drive," Tiffany says.

Mort hums, pleased. "How do you like driving?"

"I love it. It's exhilarating. It's freeing. It's . . ." She searches for a fitting word, and Mort catches my eye over her shoulder and winks.

I know he has the perfect word. And I know what it is.

High on dizziness, I laugh loudly.

Mort's smile widens at Tiffany. "It's physics."

Tiffany reclines on the video-game chair and her eyes twinkle with fondness.

Mort tosses her the keys when we leave the arcade. At the wagon, I restrain him from climbing into the passenger side. I fist his shirt and haul him into a gasping kiss.

"Yeah, I'll bite," Mort says. "What was that for?"

Everything. "Will you come to the movies with me tonight?"

He dimples. "You're asking me on a date?"

"I promise it will be good. Awesome. Epic. A real milestone."

His delight feeds into this heady feeling.

"I promise to be there."

"Good. Also, you're driving us."

Chapter Thirty-Five

MORT

I DRIVE US TO THE DRIVE-IN THEATRE AFTER STOPPING FOR FISH 'n' chips. We clutch paper-wrapped fries between our legs and pinch them out through a hole in the top. A giant chocolate milkshake sits in the console between us.

Twenty minutes into the 1978 classic *Grease*, Felix has barely said a clear sentence. He keeps looking at me and mangling his words.

I want to discuss the upcoming camping trip with Roch, but bringing up his brother on our date feels dicey.

I lift our milkshake and Felix watches me suck on the straw, mouth slackening. His desire is so beautifully blatant, I want to crawl onto him and devour him. "Any poignant facts about *Grease*?"

"Sexual. Hormones on a rampage. Men. Cars and dancing."

It's more words than he's managed since he picked me up with roses at my door, but they still don't make any sense.

"Argh." He pulls out his phone.

My phone dings. I set down the milkshake and read.

Felix: How badly is this date sucking?

Me: You nailed the greasy food and good view.

Felix: It's like. I don't know. I'm panicking. This is a DATE, Mort. A date with the man of my dreams. And I've forgotten how to speak.

I start to protest, and he cuts over me. "Normally."

I grin and type back.

Me: We've done this before, you know.

Felix: Been at a movie. I know!

Me: Dated. We just hadn't labelled it then.

Felix: Labels are making me moronic. We should trash them.

Me: Then I wouldn't get to call you my boyfriend.

Felix: Are you SURE you want to call this mumbling idiot your boyfriend?

Oh hell yes.

Me: I could stick to calling this mumbling idiot my sunshine.

His lips twitch as he stares at the lit screen.

Felix: He loves when you call him that.

Me: What's making you so nervous tonight?

Felix: Truth?

Me: Always.

Felix: I'm so completely dizzy.

I smile.

Me: Yeah, me too.

Felix: I'm also anticipating you taking my virginity when we get home.

My phone drops into the fries and I pluck it up. God, Felix. I adjust myself with a lusty hum in my throat.

Felix: *Hoping* you'll take it.

I suck in a breath. "I, yes, I uh . . ." I stop and type.

Me: Is this mumbling moronic-ness contagious? I fear you just gave it to me.

Felix: Welcome to my world.

Me: Delighted to be here.

Felix: Ohh. I just thought of something.

Me: What?

Felix: It's the height of wit.

Me: Oh, dear God.

Felix: Will you drive us home and be morty with me? Will you drive us home and be a morty, morty boy?

I dive over the console, fries landing near the gearstick, and kiss him. My laughter pebbles over his salty lips.

It isn't the height of wit. It's something better than that. It's Felix reclaiming my name with me. It's touching. "Can we speak again now?"

"We can try."

He watches the big screen as I settle back in my seat.

"What are you thinking?" I ask.

He flushes. "Drive us past the supermarket?"

Forget the rest of the movie. I drive us to Countdown and Felix tells me to stay put. He disappears inside for ten minutes and returns with bulging shorts pockets.

He snags his seatbelt into place without emptying his pockets, and points. "Go."

I spend almost as much time eyeing those bulges as I do the road, and it's a chore when I have to open the door. He scuttles inside the house and kicks off his shoes, then wavers between the living room and my bedroom.

He opts for my bedroom, and I steady my breath. After I remove my boots, I follow him.

He's stripped my bed and laid the blanket on the carpet and is messing about in my closet.

I lean against the doorframe, ankles crossed. "What are you doing?"

He pops up. "I'm gonna be blunt. Just know I'm saying this because I have feelings, okay? Your bed sucks. And those feelings I have? Mostly a sore back after two nights sleeping in here with you."

"And this set-up on the floor is your solution?"

"Only because no store is selling us a new bed at ten o'clock."

My pulse quickens at the way he says 'us' so easily, like there is no doubt I'd buy a bed with him. "We could sleep in your bed," I suggest. "Or in the back of The Groove."

He nods. "Yes, yes we could go at it in the wagon. But there's this thing called neighborhood watch, and I've had a few too many confrontations with police already."

"And your bed?"

"Look, I understand you're all sexual confidence and performance anywhere, anytime." I snort, and he continues, "But I have no idea how loud I'll be—and my sisters and mum don't need to find out at the same time. And, Mort? I have a feeling I'll be very loud."

Jesus Christ.

I adjust my straining erection that wants in on that. "What happened to panicky, monosyllabic Felix?"

"He turned into panicky, rambling Felix."

I cross to the closet and rest my arms across the shoulder-height top of the door. Felix dives into the closet again. "Want to talk about it?"

"I'm searching for your sleeping bag or another blanket for cushioning."

"I meant the panicky part."

He ducks back out, clutching swaths of black material. He tries to figure out what it is. "I'm panicky because of the whole awkward and painful thing. What if you don't enjoy it?"

Oh, that's so beyond impossible. I'm already enjoying it, and neither of us are naked yet.

I tuck a finger under his jaw. He slowly faces me. "Even if it is the most awkward sex ever, I'll enjoy it, Felix. Because it's happening with you."

He lets out a relieved breath. "Good, good. Great." He lifts the black material. "Now what on Earth is this?"

"You're holding it sideways." I throw it on, donning the hood for good measure.

He eyes me up and down like he did when I wore it on Halloween.

"I'm the Grim Reaper."

He cracks into a laugh. "Christ, take it off."

I move around the open door, hook the waist of Felix's still bulging shorts, and haul him close. "Not before I reap a few things."

"You already reaped my undying affection, a plethora of gooey smiles, and all my insecurities. What more could you possibly want?"

I eye his pockets with an arched brow. What more could I want? "What's in your pockets." I steer him against the closed closet door and run my finger under his waistline, eliciting a moan.

He cocks his hips up. "Empty them."

I sink my fingers into his right pocket, expecting to find a small squashed box of condoms. I do touch a box, only when I tug it free, it's a box of chocolates.

I toss them onto the floor-bed and dive into his pocket. Felix hums, a mischievous smirk playing at his rosy lips.

I pull out a second sampler box of chocolates and laugh. "I know you've never done this before, but you do understand the concept of protection, right?"

He hooks his arms around me. "Maybe you should do your job better."

"My job?"

"Science. Coming to better conclusions after a thorough investigation of *all* my pockets."

I slide my hands around his waist, propelling his crotch against mine as I descend toward his back pockets. "You mean my job of feeling you up?"

He rubs his erection against mine. "I love how handsy you get in the pursuit of knowledge."

I dip my fingers into his back pockets and feel familiar foiled edges. I pull out a row of condoms and Felix's gaze dances with humor, excitement, and anticipation.

"What about lube, sunshine?"

He nuzzles my neck and flicks his tongue over my ear. "You have plenty of that in your beside drawer. Now, please, please get inside me."

Chapter Thirty-Six

FELIX

"YOU'RE TENSING."

"Just checking you're paying attention to my southern bits."

"Trust me, your southern bits have all of my attention. Are you okay?"

"You'll go slowly, right?"

"You bet your ass I will."

"That's kind of what I'm betting."

Mort laughs. "Yes, Felix. I'll go slow. I'll stop if you want me to, too."

"I don't want to stop. I want you, for the purpose of this moment, to pretend I'm not this sculpted man-beast you see before you, but rather one of delicate structure."

"Okay, that does not work. Now I'm imagining you as a man-beast."

"Imagining?" I scoff, then laugh when Mort lightly bites

the curve of my neck. His lubed fingers slip in and out of me, and in—darting over my prostate. I moan.

"That opens you up."

"Forget everything I said. Get in me. Hurry up."

Mort slides on a condom and slathers lube over himself. He positions himself at my entrance and stares down at me, besotted and trembling with desire. He claims my lips and I wrap my arms around his neck, gasping into his mouth when his cock breaches me.

"You okay?" he asks, panting to keep in control.

I kiss him again. "Yes."

He pushes in, filling me, spearing me. His hand wraps around my flagging cock and strokes me hard, strokes me until I squirm under him for more.

He rocks gently, kissing the corner of my lips. I like how close Mort is to me. How his muscles strain as he holds himself over me. I lick the light sheen of sweat at his shoulder and clavicle. He groans and lengthens his thrusts.

The friction over my prostate unfurls sensation toward every inch of my body. I feel it in the heels of my feet that rub against the blankets, my thighs where Mort's legs comb mine on every instroke, my hips that tingle from the puffs of air we create, my nipples that bump against the hairs on his chest, my neck where he loves to suck and bite.

My cock rubs against his stomach, leaking precome—any tenderness in my ass has dissolved. God, this feels good. This feels right. This feels like it'll be over too soon.

I try to pull out of the mounting sensations, just enough to prolong the delicious build-up. Mort's eyes lock onto mine. His guttural grunts combined with the restrained power of his thrusts throw me over the damn edge.

I give into the escalating pleasure, muttering curses and words like *more* and *harder*. My body loosens. My head falls back, my knees spread wide, my fingers claw at him, urging him *faster.*

He struggles to keep in control, and I cry for him to lose it. To give it to me.

He collapses onto me, sucks my lip, bites my neck, murmurs in my ear how fucking tight I am. When I bite his neck, he loses it. He hooks my leg over his shoulder and pistons a hundred *yeses* out of me.

I'm flushed and needy yet awed at how easy sex is with Mort, how perfectly compatible we feel.

I grab my aching cock and jerk it fast, staring blatantly at Mort as I have always done, and he stares back.

My jaw clenches as my orgasm consumes me. Mort pounds into me as I spill and spill and spill.

He buries himself deep and his cock pulses inside me as he cries out. He is insanely hot with his face twisted in pleasure and his body shuddering.

I brace his shaking arms through his orgasm and steer him against me when he's done. His slackened weight is heavy and warm. His heart thunders over mine.

He lifts just enough to scroll my face and catalogue how I'm feeling. He dips his lips to my curved ones. "You're smirking."

"You're smoldering."

Mort's crooked smile has me lifting up and snatching a kiss.

"How do you feel?" He slides out of me and rolls to my side.

"Right now, empty." I turn onto my side and tap our noses together. His eyes crinkle. "But before, delightfully full."

Mort removes the condom, ties it, and tosses it on the naked bed. I burrow against his chest. I breathe him in, marveling at what we just shared. Marveling at the prospect of a lifetime of this. Mort and me. In this house that we'll reclaim until it is ours. We'll have an open-door policy where our family can visit as they please. We'll need three bedrooms. Two of the kids will have to share, but we'll make it work.

One big crazy family.

I sigh through Mort's chest hair. "You should go camping with Roch."

His chin moves against the top of my head. "What?"

"He's your best friend."

Mort pulls back and looks at me. "Felix, I—"

"No. You need all the love in your life, and Roch loves you too. So don't hold back, okay? Just don't tell him . . . you know."

Mort lifts a challenging brow. "You know . . . what?"

"That we're . . ." I swat his arm. "Don't tell him. We'll do it together when you get back."

"Not before I leave?"

"You're heading into the bush. Anything could happen and he could claim it an accident."

"Good call." Mort laughs, curls a hand around my nape, and kisses me. "Now, open up."

"I thought I just did?"

"Your *mouth*."

Mort slips a morsel of chocolate that he somehow procured over my bottom lip. Dark flavor with a hint of vanilla bursts over my tongue. "Oh my God, could this night get any better?"

Mort leans in and whispers into my ear. "You know that Christmas when you told me true love would feel like sunshine?"

"Yes," I croak against his neck, heart hammering.

"And you know how I always call you sunshine?"

My "yes" is a rasp.

He pulls back and looks into my eyes.

I melt.

Chapter Thirty-Seven

MORT

The moist air clings to my skin with the scent of pine and mud.

Roch stirs next to me on the log where we ate dinner, hunched in jackets. Our single tents are set up behind us. One more night, and we drive back to Wellington.

Roch studies his interlaced hands, tapping his thumbs like he wants to say something.

"What's up, Roch?"

He glances at me and out toward the night-heavy bush silhouetted against a navy sky. "Felix told me you know he's gay."

I still—except for my heart. That thumps like it's in a boxing match. I've been avoiding conversations about Felix all weekend, even though all I want to do is tell my best friend that I've bloody well met the love of my life.

But. Telling Felix's brother is something we have to do

together.

Roch shoulder-checks me. "You do know, right? I didn't fuck up?"

I have to be careful here. "Yeah, I know."

Not wanting to encourage the topic further, I fake a stretch and push myself off the log.

Roch catches my eye. "So, do you know other gay or bisexual guys like me?"

"A few," I say, collecting our dinner bowls and utensils.

"Good guys?"

"Sure."

"Any who are single?"

I almost drop the bowls and forks but catch them roughly against my thighs. "Please don't tell me you're calling the wedding off."

"What? Never. I'm in love with Lauren. I wanted to talk about Felix."

I calmly stack our cups into the bowls, my heart whacking about. "What about him?"

"Maybe you could introduce him to some of your gay acquaintances?"

"Uh . . ." *How about not?*

"I don't want him to be lonely. I don't think he's ever really dated. He might still be a virgin—"

"Stop." I scrub my face, trying to kill the sudden sensual images of Felix as he came with my cock buried deep in him. "Felix can navigate his own relationships."

"Have you seen him trying to flirt—other than with you?"

I'm transported back to the gay bar and the following day when he tried to flirt with Jason from work. "He's charming and quick-witted once he gets comfortable with someone."

"He's like a cub butting up against a tiger. I can't believe you aren't agreeing with me."

"Maybe the right guy will love his flirting anxiety. Ever consider that?"

"Huh, some people find that attractive?"

"Look, even tiger cubs have stripes—and they learn to roar real quick."

Roch grins. "You have so much faith in my brother."

So much love, too. "Can we quit talking about matching up your brother?"

"Testy."

"I'm tired."

"All right," he says, standing up. "Pass me the dishes and get some shuteye."

I pass him the dishes, but not much shuteye happens.

I toss and turn in my pup tent and scramble for my phone and portable charger when it beeps shortly after six in the morning. I sink back into my sleeping bag.

Felix: Hey.

Me: Good morning.

Felix: I'm so done. Barely slept.

Me: Barely?

Felix: Barely.

Me: Vivid description. I can imagine you bare—and I'm fairly sure it explains why you didn't sleep.

Felix: While you might be alone in your pup tent, the twins are looking over my shoulders.

Me: Lol, right then. They're up early.

Felix: They're wondering if you and I would race their go-karts down the street.

Me: Why us?

Felix: Because they don't want to crash and end up in hospital. Their words.

Me: How charming.

Felix: They're lucky they're funny.

Me: :-D When?

Felix: Today, when you come back with Roch. Mum wants to watch too.

Me: An audience and everything.

Felix: Twins are gone . . . I'm hoping you'll create an excuse for both of us. I'm worried the karts will break under our weight.

Me: They won't.

Felix: How do you know?

Me: I helped build them.

Felix: Quite sure of ourselves, aren't we?

Me: I'm a teacher, a man with an honors degree in physics and chemistry, a—let's call me a smart man.

Felix: A smart man. A smart ass . . . So, no getting us out of the go-karts?

Me: No, but . . .

Felix: But?

Me: If you end up with a chafed backside because I forgot everything I studied at uni, I'll . . .

Felix: You'll . . . ???!!!

Me: Are you alone, sunshine?

Felix: *Barely*.

I laugh aloud. God, I miss him.

I flip open my sleeping bag and grip myself.

Me: Let me tell you exactly how I'd kiss you better . . .

An hour later, I've packed my tramping pack and I'm battling my tent into its ridiculously undersized bag.

Roch emerges from his tent with a yawn, like he's had the best sleep of his life. "Eager to get home, huh?"

Oh yeah. "Figure we should beat traffic."

He approaches hesitantly. "Are we good?"

"Of course."

"Sorry about last night. I didn't mean to make you feel like you have to help Felix. You're right. He's an adult, he can work these things out for himself."

I stop fighting the zip. "No, it's not that I don't want to help. Just . . ." I look at him squarely. "He's fine, Roch."

Roch nods and his eyes widen. I follow his gaze to where a kea is pinching the lunch container I'd prepared for our road trip home.

We watch, fascinated, as he takes it apart.

I yank the last bit of my zip in place and sling my tent to my bulging pack. "There goes the food. We'll have to stop at McDonalds."

Roch laughs. "I'm not sure this whole thing wasn't planned. You love greasy food."

I eye Roch's tent. "Let's get you packed up. I'm hungry." And ready to hit the road.

Five hours and only one McDonald's stop later, we park The Groove outside the Rochesters', behind Roch's car.

We climb out, limbs stiff from sitting all day, and laboriously move Roch's gear to his car.

We stand between our two vehicles. Roch claps my bicep. "Great weekend, thanks."

"Yeah, I enjoyed myself."

"Definitely something to repeat. Maybe without the fall down the muddy bank."

"Or getting stung by a wasp and bitching about it for an hour."

Roch mocks being offended. "It was not an hour."

"No. It was two."

We laugh easily. For the first time in months, it feels like we've truly slotted back into our old friendship.

"Maybe without phones next time?" Roch chides gently. "You were on yours every time you got a single bar of coverage."

"Yeah, I was."

"Shit. You've met someone, haven't you?"

I quirk him a brow. "You're quite the Sherlock."

"Who is he?"

Thankfully at that moment, April and May bounce out of the house.

"Mort! Roch! Finally. Go-kart time." They gesture to the go-karts waiting in the front yard. "We've been waiting *all morning.*"

May pounces on Roch, tugging his arm, while April yells for Mum to come watch.

"You have to watch with us," May says to Roch. "And Mum made chicken lasagna for lunch."

Chicken lasagna? Dolores cooked my favorite.

April prods my side. "You use my go-kart, okay?"

I laugh. "All right, all right. Where are we doing this?"

"From there," she says, pointing toward the end of the cul-de-sac, a good half kilometer away, "to past The Groove."

It's straight all the way. Good thing too, especially for our test race.

May swaps me a bike helmet for my cap. "Put this on and drag the go-kart up there."

"Demanding, aren't they?" Felix's creamy voice wafts from behind me.

I whisk around. His bright blue eyes dance at the sight of me and his lips turn up into a sexy, secret smile. He's wearing shorts and a button-up shirt open at the collar and his hair looks like he might have spent a good portion of the morning lounging in bed.

My hands twitch to pull him into me, but Roch's presence at our side forces me painfully backward. "Felix." Missed me? "How've you been?"

April jams a helmet onto his head. Felix winces. "Chat later," she says. "To the end of the street. Go."

Felix scowls playfully at April and then nods for us to jump in the go-karts.

There's no arguing with single-minded ten-year-olds.

Chapter Thirty-Eight

FELIX

Mort and I test our vehicles as we drive to the starting point. My bright blue go-kart has a white bow tie painted on the hood, Mort's is a blazing red. The accelerator is sensitive and the lightest touch has May's baby revving. I test the brake. Smooth. Mort and the girls did a stellar job.

Mort zooms ahead. A rush of giddiness hits me every time I see him. He's back. I missed him. It's been strange sleeping in my own bed again. Not that Mort would have objected if I'd crashed at his place. I would've too, if not for the sad state of his bed.

Maybe if we finish this race quickly and scoff lunch, we'll have the afternoon to shop for a new one.

I turn the go-kart around and line up next to Mort. "I hope you're not tired. I have plans for you."

Mort's eyes hit mine with a blaze of amusement under his

dark helmet. "Are you torturing me to gain an edge in this race?"

"Now there's an idea. Mort?" I say, adjusting my helmet more firmly onto my head. "Watch me ride this thing like I will you later. Hard and fast."

"You're killing me."

"Well, *Mort.* Turnabout's fair play."

April and May unwind Mum of her olive scarf, where she stands at the rear of The Groove.

Once they have it, they drag Roch to the middle of the street and stretch his arms wide. I'm not sure if it's to stop non-existent traffic, but if it is . . . I groan. "Roch is a literal road-block. That better not be symbolic."

Mort taps his wheel. "Of course it's symbolic."

"What?" I splutter.

He grins. "He's the last roadblock before we can truly be us."

May races up to us, scarf flying about her face. Grinning, she steps in the space between our go-karts. "First to Roch wins," she calls, hands cupped around her mouth, scarf almost whipping out of her grip.

She grabs it and holds it above her head.

"Ready for this?" Mort murmurs to me.

I narrow my eyes on Roch. "I have a suspended license that backs me up when I say speed is my middle name."

Mort snorts, and I wave him my middle finger.

"*Ready,*" May yells.

Mort lifts a challenging brow and revs his engine.

"*Get set.*"

I smile as May swishes the scarf dramatically down, and toss Mort some go-kart-stalling words. "I love you, Mort. I've loved you forever."

"*Go.*"

I press down on the accelerator and roar past May down

the street, wind whipping in my face. Houses and parked cars blur, and Roch, April, and Mum grow bigger.

Halfway, I catch a flash of red out the corner of my eye. Holy crap, Mort's catching up. And with a vengeance.

I press harder on the accelerator, and the steering wobbles. I swerve toward the middle of the street and lessen my foot on the gas to correct.

Mort inches closer and closer.

Roch thinks better of standing in the middle of the road and races to the sidewalk, tackling a by-standing April out of our way.

The engine hums, vibrating around my thighs. Mort levels with me and I tap the accelerator once more, passing The Groove first by a foot.

I hit the brakes a little too hard and swerve as I slow. Mort's kart bumps into mine and we skid to a halt together the last meters.

I'm vibrating with adrenalin and the high of winning, and I'm laughing hard.

Mort glares at me, but its effect is ruined by his twitching lips. "You played dirty."

"Is it dirty when it's the truth?"

Mort's lips curve higher—not his usual halfway grin, but a face-splitting smile that makes him glow.

Roch approaches, chuckling, arms folded. "You guys okay?"

"Yes." I answer, scrolling every inch of Mort I can see to check for injuries. "You good?"

His eyes flicker softly, held on me. "Yeah, the best."

Roch shifts before our go-karts as Mort reaches a hand to the side of mine. "Felix?"

"Yes," I say breathlessly.

He leans in, whispering. "Want to talk to your brother?"

I gulp. "Nope?"

Mort inclines his head and draws back. "Okay, then."

I pull myself out of the go-kart and drop my helmet on the seat, and Mort does the same. He steps onto the pavement, and I grab him by the elbow. "Mort?"

He raises a brow, and I hook him closer to my side and pull him around to face a frowning Roch. "Let's talk to my brother."

Chapter Thirty-Nine

MORT

ROCH STARES AT OUR JOINED ARMS. "WHAT'S GOING ON?"

Felix rolls his shoulders back and sidles closer to me. "We have something to share with you."

I've known Roch all my life, but I have no idea how he'll react. I'm faking confidence for Felix's sake, but a tremor runs down my arm and I'm sure Felix feels it against his.

"Something special," I say, voice scratchy. Felix breaks his focus from Roch briefly to give me a reassuring smile.

"Yes, very special."

Roch's expression flickers with surprise and shadows over with hurt and disappointment. "Maybe one of you wants to tell me before I start making it up?"

Felix stutters. "S-so. The thing is, you were always going to be the hardest one to tell. And we wanted to tell you together." He swallows and I thread my fingers through his. "This won't change things between you and Mort. I love that he has you in his life even if I've worried. What I'm awkwardly trying to say is: we're together. Mort's my boyfriend."

When he says boyfriend, my apprehension shifts. Instant fondness tickles over my body like goosebumps. I squeeze his hand and begin to speak when Roch cuts over me, staring hard at Felix.

"He's my best friend."

"Yes, Roch, I am," I say. "But I don't think you've quite understood—"

"You're sleeping together?"

"It's more than that—"

"Yeah, you're boyfriends. You're sleeping together *regularly*." Roch shuts his eyes and covers a hand over them.

"Look, Roch—"

He pinches the bridge of his nose and cuts me off for a third time. "You should have told me this weekend."

"We wanted to do it together."

Roch whips his betrayed expression to Felix and it deepens. "When we went shopping and I opened up to you? Why didn't you tell me then?"

"Roch . . ."

He throws his hands up. "I don't care who of you, but either my best friend or my brother might have told me instead of leaving me to make an idiot of myself unearthing my emotions. Well. I guess I know where I stand now."

His words bite. "I'm sorry. I'm truly sorry if it hurts, but it's true. Felix comes first, he'll always come first. I'm in love with him."

I don't struggle to identify the flash of pain over his face, but I struggle with causing it. I don't want to hurt him, but he has to know—they both have to know—where I stand with Felix.

"Say something, please."

"I've got to go."

"You told the girls you'd stay for lunch," Felix attempts.

"I'm no longer hungry."

I try and fail to hook his gaze. "So you're just leaving?"

"Probably best."

"Don't you want to, if not congratulate us, at least talk about it?"

A cool breeze stirs between us, thankfully pushing Felix's soft, clean scent to my nose. I have him at my side. That matters most.

Still, my belly swoops with disappointment.

Dolores sidles into view, hair fraying around her bun, eyes prickling with tears. She'd overheard us, then. She knows too.

She slides an arm around Roch's, mirroring Felix and me, and my heart punches my chest. Is she taking sides?

She speaks in his ear, pats him and lets go.

I frown as she steps to us. She's eyeing me. "Oh, Mort."

"Dolores."

She touches my arm and rubs. "I knew you two were together, but in love?"

I steel my jaw. I've forgiven Dolores for many things, but if she dares to even suggest she's unhappy with this, she'll lose me forever. "My heart is hitched for good."

Felix's arm tightens at my side and he makes a gulping sound. I take his hand, threading our fingers and pressing our clammy palms together. He pumps my hand and I'm ready for anything Dolores has to say.

Her smile wobbles. "Well that's . . ." She swallows and straightens. "That's wonderful."

Wonderful?

I blink, unprepared for that response—

She pulls me into a hug, my hand still attached to Felix's. "You couldn't have fallen in love with anyone more deserving. I'm happy for you."

I slowly pull back. "You won't try to cast me out of the family again?"

"I have a lot to make up for. I know, and I'm sorry. I want to work on my relationship with you. With all of you. Just like you've taught me."

I can't believe what I'm hearing. "Really?"

"You were like a son to me, Mort. The songs, the smart-mouthed replies, the pride I had when you played soccer . . . You've always been amazing—you never changed—that was me. And I don't like the woman I became. I loved you as my son, and I want to continue loving you as my son. If it's not too late?"

I study her sincere, hopeful expression. My voice is quiet, but I know she and Felix can hear. "Felix gave you life. It looks like you're finally starting to live it."

"I am. I will."

"I love him, Dolores. I *love* him."

She nods and backs away, and Felix curls closer.

Roch slinks up, frowning at me. "Do you really?" Genuine concern shades his voice. "Or is this the next best thing if you couldn't have me?"

Ouch.

Felix flinches and trembles. This is his worst insecurity tossed out into the open. Fuck. I wish I could prove my feelings—

"He does love me," Felix says quietly, eyes locking on his brother. "Ask me how I know."

Roch hesitates and I'm one pent-breath from asking myself. "How do you know?" Roch asks.

"He drops me to work and picks me up every day—even on his holidays. He takes me out to bars when I ask him to, he drives me places over the rainbow when I'm having a hard day. He always shows me I come first." He pauses to take a breath and continues quieter, "Like when I overheard you on the bridge, telling him about yourself. He ran to reassure me I'm the one he wants as his boyfriend. Like when I lied about kicking your ass at Dance Dance Revolution and—"

Roch frowns. "You lied? But I saw your score—"

"Mort danced under my name. He danced until he beat both your old scores. He danced for me . . ." He chokes on his words, gaze burning lovingly into mine.

Ah, Felix. I'd do it all over again.

Roch looks startled. "You did that?"

I don't look away from Felix. "I wish I could prove you're my number one."

"This is . . ." Roch rubs his nape. "I've been acting like a jealous dick."

Felix clears his throat. "That's okay, Roch. It runs in the family."

Roch laughs, and I wrap my arm around Felix's shoulders. He slides his arm around my waist.

"Oh, fuck, I get it," Roch says, shaking his head. "This is why you didn't want an invite to my wedding. You want Felix to bring you as his plus one."

"And be seated at your table, yeah."

Felix shakes his head at me. "What if I hadn't wanted to be boyfriends?"

Thank God that isn't the case. I kiss his temple. "Then I'd be a hell of a downer at the kids' table."

Roch's lips approach an awed smile. "You really love him." Not a question this time.

I clap his shoulder. "This is what I've been saying. Though in this case, I really don't mind repeating myself." I drop my arm and shift to face Felix, nose to nose. "I love you, Felix." His smile is all-encompassing, awed, and it sparkles in his eyes and flushed cheeks. I lean in and whisper. "What's your position on kissing in front of your brother?'

Felix grabs my shirt and hauls me into a fiery kiss. "I love you, Mort."

He sinks his fingers into my helmet-matted hair and tugs me closer still. He's shaking, just a little, and I wrap my arms around him, whispering "ah, sunshine" in his ear.

Roch murmurs, "Wow, okay. If there was even a little bit of toad in you, Mort, this kiss is making you a prince."

Felix chuckles against my lips and pulls back. "So, what do you think, Roch?"

"I'll, um, stay for lunch after all."

I roll my eyes. "About us."

He measures us together for a long beat, expression flickering through emotions, and then smiles. "I know a happily ever after when I see one."

Felix and I speak at the same time, into another kiss. "So do I."

Chapter Forty

Two and a half months later . . .

FELIX

"ARGHH!"

"Is there a reason you tackled the sheets on the way out of bed?"

"Clumsy," I say, voice muffled by cotton. I sit up. Mort stops before me, freshly showered, towel wrapped loosely around his hips. His hair drips, and the droplets track through the matted hair plastered against his chest. My gaze drops lower and so does my mouth.

Two months together—living with him in the villa, breaking in our bed together—and I still can't believe how gorgeous he is. How I'm the one allowed to explore every inch of him with my mouth, with my body. And—

Stop. No time for this.

A flurry of nerves replaces the shiver of lust. "Help me out?

"Always." He pulls me up effortlessly and swoops in for a kiss. "What's got you so jumpy?"

"Roch's getting married today. Married."

"The way you're flustering, you'd think it was our wedding day."

Ha! "Oh, well . . . we can never get married. There's a real chance I might crap my pants." I shut my eyes and shake my head. "I just ruined the romance, didn't I?"

Mort laughs, loud and hearty. "We'll get married one day."

"Did you hear the bit about the pants?"

His half-cocked smirk will be the death of me. "I don't give a shit."

I start stripping out of Mort's sleep T-shirt. "So, was that you asking?"

"Unofficially. I intend to make it more memorable."

"I thought every moment with me was memorable?"

"It is." Mort shoves a hand through his hair. He falls over the twisted sheets, overcorrects, and lands on his ass with a curse. "Help me out?"

I take his hand, but he doesn't pull himself up. He turns my hand over and kisses my knuckles. "Will you marry me?"

Holy fuck. Butterflies are cleaving me in two. "Just to check, you realize you're asking after only two months, right? I still have another week before I get my license reinstated."

"We've been a lifetime in the making, and I'd love to continue making a life with you."

"I want that too. But I still stand by the possibility of crapping my pants."

"That wasn't a clear yes."

Mort tugs me onto him and despite our rush, we melt against one another—and then into one another.

Forty minutes later, after a hurried shower, I jerk into my suit. "I can't find my bow tie."

Mort watches me lazily from the bed, hand tucked behind his head, dressed in a dashing suit—sans jacket. "How do you feel about wearing one again?"

"Ready. Truly ready. If I could only find it."

"Come here."

"If we start with that again, we'll definitely be late."

"Come here," he says again, swinging his legs off the bed.

Compelled, I go to him.

He tugs me onto his lap so I'm sitting in profile to him. From under the pillows, he pulls out a wrapped gift. "Open it."

I rip into it.

A delicate wooden bow tie tumbles to my thighs. I scoop it up with an appreciative gasp. Caramel, rustic pine with gently curved edges and a silky-smooth finish. "Mort, this is beautiful."

"It was supposed to be for Christmas, but I didn't want to give you something you weren't ready for."

"I'm ready. But this is too beautiful."

"Like the person it's made for."

"You made this. For me."

He shrugs. "The wood I found at the entrance to the glow-worm cave. The moment I held it, I knew what it would be. I grabbed my knife and began whittling out a design."

"You? Whittling?" I sneak a hand over the curve of his inner thigh where his scar sits. His muscles jump. "After the last time?"

Mort's lips hop. "I admit, I thought of that moment as I worked. I thought even more of the one in your bedroom after Roch's engagement party. Your hand branded my thigh and my thoughts, Felix."

I press my lips against his, branding him again. Letting him brand me, again.

His fingers lift my shirt collar.

"Not quite tearing my shirt off, Mort. But I suppose there isn't time."

He laughs. "Roch has been hiding the bow tie for me since you moved in. He showed it to Lauren and they insisted you wear it to their wedding. I changed the neckband to match their silver color scheme."

"God, Mort. I'm going to outshine the groom."

"Yeah."

Mort unlatches the band and slides it around my collar, gaze flickering from it to me. I touch his wrist, stilling him, and rub my thumb at the base of his palm. "Yes," I breathe out and Mort swells with light. "I'm happy to tie the knot with you, Mort."

Tiffany waits for me outside our home. Dressed in a sleek black pantsuit with a rose at her breast pocket and a flat cap, she's pacing in front of The Groove, which is adorned with painted tin cans.

I break away from Mort's side. Mort greets my green-gowned mum up the path.

"Love the suit, Tiff."

She halts. "I figured if I'm chauffeuring Lauren to her wedding, I better look smart."

"The cap is a cute touch."

She glances Mort's way. "Mimicking the best in the chauffeuring business."

"So, there's this one con on your *Should I Learn to Drive* list that I want to help you with."

She looks confused. I repeat myself.

"I'm feeling more pro about driving," Tiffany says. "Well, I'm a little nervous with a bride next to me, but uh, it'll be fine.

It'll be just fine."

I pinch the tip of her cap fondly. "It will be fine, Tiff."

She wrings her hands. "The bride is waiting for me. You need to give me the keys to the Groove and get to the beach with Mum and Mort."

"Okay, I have the keys somewhere."

She looks about ready to murder me. "Somewhere? You better know exactly where. The bride can be fashionably late, not 'had to walk' late."

I hide a grin. "Maybe it's this pocket . . ."

"You're doing this on purpose."

I draw the keys out from inside my jacket. "Aha. Here they are."

She grabs them. "Thanks—hey, these look different."

"Yes, yes they do."

She inspects them. "It has a new key chain with my name on it." Her head snaps up and our eyes meet. "Why does it have a new key chain with my name on it?"

"This is the con I want to help you with. The Groove is yours. Now you don't have to spend your money on a vehicle."

"You're kidding me."

"That'd be a mean joke."

"This is for real?"

"For real." Mort passed it on to me once; passing it on to Tiffany feels right.

She stares, bewildered, at the keys. "What about you?"

"We're looking into getting something together. He wants a hearse, but I'm trying to persuade him to find something a touch less conspicuous."

She laughs. "You won't get pulled over as much in a hearse. It'll save you from having to 'charm' the officers."

"Good grief, you're probably right. A hearse it is."

Tiffany launches herself at me and we stumble back. I find my footing and hug her back. "Thank you, Felix. You're the best." She taps just under my bow tie. "Now get out of here. We have a wedding to get to."

~

THE CEREMONY IS A TOUCHING, SIMPLE AFFAIR ALONG THE beach at low tide. We cheer the married couple, take staged photos along the rock pools, and dip our feet in cool salty water as we dance our way toward the rustic hall that hosts the reception.

The food is delicious, and after my speech wishing the bride and groom all the love in the world, I enjoy myself even more.

Mum surprises us with a touching song—not even off-tune —and we learn she's been secretly taking lessons. April and May tinker with bubbles and experiments for the kids, and then we're all surrounding the polished dance floor as my brother and his wife take their first dance.

"Look at them," Mort says admiringly. His arm brushes mine with an addictive spark of electricity. "It's like they're . . ."

"Professionals?"

That earns me an amused eye roll. "Floating."

I point toward the stage set up beside the dance floor.

"I don't get why there's a piano and an electric guitar when the "band" is a single guy playing this tune from a record."

"It's the record from their first proper date—from Lauren's vinyl collection."

"You'd think my brother might share these tidbits with me."

"I found out from Lauren."

I laugh, and then sigh as I watch the happy couple float.

When their dance ends, applause trumpets. When the DJ leaves, Mort jumps onstage, congratulates the bride and groom for their spectacular footwork, and dares any of us to compete with that.

He swivels to Roch and Lauren. He's not looking at me, but I can feel his attention blasting my way. "My gift to the newlyweds. Roch, thank you for keeping this a surprise for your beautiful wife."

Lauren gives my brother a baffled smile, and Mort grins. "Let's turn up the music."

Two men jog on stage and Lauren and I scream. It's Pax Polo and his husband—band manager and sometimes musical partner—Clifford Wilson.

Holy crap.

I can't believe my eyes. I can't believe my ears!

Mort jogs down from the stage. I meet him at the base of the stairs with a grip that might juice his biceps.

"Pax Polo?"

"I told you I take greasing you up seriously."

Pax Polo sings softly into the microphone accompanied by Cliff playing the piano.

Roch dances with Mum, Lauren with her dad. I'm a quivering, over-excited, love-struck mess. "Would you like to dance with me?"

Mort's expression shifts into surprise. "You're asking me? I thought I'd have to lure you onto the dance floor."

"Consider me well and truly and forever lured."

I stride toward the shiny floor, turn back and hold my arm out for him.

Mort's smile holds the world as he takes my hand, and we dance.

~ The End ~

Acknowledgments

I couldn't have written this book without the rock-solid support of my hubby. You are an amazing dad, and I love navigating this parental adventure with you. As always, you are my inspiration for writing romance. You set a high bar, love.

Vir, Sunne, Lynda. Thank you for all your tremendous guidance to help shape this story—and thank you for your patience with me. This script saw many changes over the months.

Cheers to HJS Editing for all the fantastic edits and the fast turn-around. And thank you to Lynda Lamb for proofreading, and Vicki for being a wonderful final eyes reader.

Lastly, big thank you to Natasha for designing the cover. I love that we found an image of two guys dancing—it's perfect.

Anyta Sunday

HEART-STOPPING SLOW BURN

A bit about me: I'm a big, BIG fan of slow-burn romances. I love to read and write stories with characters who slowly fall in love.

Some of my favorite tropes to read and write are: Enemies to Lovers, Friends to Lovers, Clueless Guys, Bisexual, Pansexual, Demisexual, Oblivious MCs, Everyone (Else) Can See It, Slow Burn, Love Has No Boundaries.

I write a variety of stories, Contemporary MM Romances with a good dollop of angst, Contemporary lighthearted MM Romances, and even a splash of fantasy.
My books have been translated into German, Italian, French, Spanish, and Thai.

Contact: http://www.anytasunday.com/about-anyta/
Sign up for Anyta's newsletter and receive a free e-book: http://www.anytasunday.com/newsletter-free-e-book/

www.ingramcontent.com/pod-product-compliance
Lightning Source LLC
La Vergne TN
LVHW091403190726
843491LV00006B/1235